Champion Chocolatier
Reality Bites

Amanda Zieba

Published by Amanda Zieba, Kindle Direct Press
www.amandazieba.com
Copyright 2019

Dedicated

to my friend, and real-life Food Network Holiday Baking Champion (twice!), Jen Barney.

(Photo credit: Food Network)

Thank you for letting borrow inspiration from your personal journey and success. I wish you nothing but the best and hope that more sweet rewards await you in the future.

*Learn more about Jen at **www.meringuecakes.com**.*

More books by Amanda Zieba

<u>For Adults</u>
Champion Chocolatier

<u>*For Children and Young Adults*</u>
Pauly Wants to Doodle All the Day
Orphan Train Riders
The Birthday Cache
Breaking the Surface
Bridging the Tides

<u>*Learn to Write*</u>
Under Construction: A Young Writer's Workbook
Story Seedlings: A Six Week Independent Writing Program

<u>*Coming Soon*</u>
The Bigfoot Blunder: A Theo Geo Adventure
(KWiL Publishing, Spring 2020)

January 23

Chapter 1

Emmy sneezed. Two hundred million virus particles spread faster than a bullet train from her nostrils into the air space surrounding her bed. She was thankful to not be in her kitchen contaminating everything in sight, and simultaneously wishing she hadn't let Eddie talk her into watching that epidemic documentary last night on Netflix. It was one thing to feel sick, but another thing entirely to know the scientific effect of every cough, sneeze, and sinus twinge. Emmy lay back down on her pillow and wondered how there was room for all of these thoughts in her head when it felt like sludgy mucous occupied every available millimeter of her body from the neck up.

She glanced at the clock: 7:13 a.m. For small-business owners, sick days were nonexistent. During tourist season Emmy worked every day. The past year had seen enough success that she was able to hire a few part-time employees though, so Emmy reached for her phone and texted the most reliable one. After securing Jenna to come into work and texting Rachel the updated employee roster for the day, she swallowed two gel caps promising quick relief and collapsed back into bed.

Emmy woke hours later, still unable to breathe through her nose. Obscuring the view of her clock were a tall cup of to-go coffee and a cranberry orange muffin. Eddie had scrawled a note.

Rest up. I'll see you after work. Feel better soon!
Love,
Eddie

P.S. Remember that your sneeze particles can travel up to twenty feet, so if you could contain your sickness just to our bedroom that would cut down on my cleaning time tonight. Thanks, hun!

Emmy propped herself up in bed, took a drink of the lukewarm coffee, and reached for her phone to text Eddie a thank-you. But an email notification froze her hand, leaving it hovering over the smooth glass surface of the screen. Emmy blinked twice. Maybe she was hallucinating? Maybe she had taken too many cold medicine capsules? But no, despite clearing her groggy vision, the message was still there.

YOU HAVE BEEN SELECTED.

Emmy swiped at the screen and opened the email.

Congratulations!

You have been selected to compete in the Vanderbilt Valentine's Day Candy-Making Competition! Eight talented candy makers from around the country will be competing on live TV for the chance to win $100,000. To sweeten the deal, *the winner will also secure a traditional publishing contract with EatTV for a cookbook. Just imagine, a cookbook featuring fabulous YOU and your recipes. Each contestant will be expected to spend two weeks at the Vanderbilt Estates (Biltmore) for the filming of the show, to sign insurance and press release waivers, and to complete the contestant questionnaire. (Additional duties may be added upon the discretion of the producer.)*

A camera crew and our host, Pierce Beaumont, will arrive at your store at 2 p.m. on Tuesday, January 23rd. Please be ready to give us a tour of your store and have a selected treat ready for tasting.

We look forward to meeting you in person and wish you the best of luck in this exciting competition. Remember, life is as sweet as you make it!

Sincerely,
Dixie Champlain
EatTV Executive Producer

Emmy read the message through twice. Then she leapt from the bed and danced, her knees and arms a wild and uncoordinated flurry of extreme happiness.

And then she coughed, hard. The blunt force of her sickness knocked her backward to her bed, where she sat down violently hacking at the phlegm in her throat. She grabbed a Kleenex and blew her nose.

Emmy remembered the day she submitted her application for the competition. She had come back to the store after being completely blown off at the Chamber of Commerce. She had stopped in to talk to someone about providing dessert for the next monthly Learn and Lunch. With each individually wrapped sweet Emmy planned to put a little flyer with a coupon for holiday goods on business orders for employee gifts. It would be a great way to network and plant seeds for potential business. But when she talked to the woman in charge of the educational lunch program, she had no idea who Emmy was.

"I'm sorry, dear, which business do you own?" the woman had asked Emmy.

"Sweet Shores Chocolate Store, down in Canal Park," Emmy said, her confidence starting to waver.

"I thought Mr. Edwards retired?" she questioned again.

"Yes, he did," Emmy tried to explain patiently. "But I reopened the store about a month later. Same name. New owner. Me! Emmy Dawson Dawson." Emmy stuck out her hand to officially greet the woman on the other side of the counter.

"Oh, yes!" The woman's eyes lit up with recognition. "I know you. We met at Taste of Duluth this summer. You're Eddie's girlfriend."

"Ah, yes," Emmy said, taken aback that this was her claim to fame. "I am."

"Oh, I just love that boy. I mean, he's not a boy anymore, but he was, when I first met him. I think I'll always remember him as a squirt hockey player missing his two front teeth. Gosh, that was ages ago."

Emmy stood there, not sure what to say, so she nodded.

"Please tell him I say hello," the woman

continued and flashed Emmy her name tag.

"Brenda. From the Chamber. And give him one of these. We'd love for him to speak at a Lunch and

Learn, or one of our Chamber Skills Series classes."

Brenda loaded Emmy's hands full of brochures and flyers about the Chamber's opportunities to network and connect and then wished her well. A minute later Emmy was on the stoop of the Chamber building unsure of what had just happened. She'd gone in to get a gig for herself, and left with business for Eddie instead. She hadn't been rejected as much as she had been invisible.

She knew it was irrational to be annoyed with Eddie. But she was. What did being cute and a hockey player have to do with running a good business? It shouldn't matter. But apparently, in a small town, it did.

Emmy stormed back into Sweet Shores and gave Rachel an earful.

"Can you believe it?" she raged as she whisked a bowl of eggs, a tad too vigorously.

"Yes, I can. Emmy, despite the progress our country has made in the last one hundred years, we still live in a patriarchy."

"Well, that sucks."

"You're right. It does." Rachel looked at her with an arched eyebrow. "So what are you gonna do about it?"

Emmy put the batter she'd been making in the refrigerator and slammed the door.

"Something big."

It had taken her a few days to find the right opportunity. But after scouring the internet and

(sigh) reading the Chamber materials and even
looking through her alma matter's alumni news
section for leads on how other grads had earned
notoriety and fame, she'd come up with the answer.
A contest, an award, a competition. That was the
answer.

A few hours of fruitful internet searching filled
in the missing details. The Vanderbilt Valentine's
Day Candy-Making Competition. It took a few more
days to complete the application materials, including
several customer reviews, a sample menu of her
best candies, pictures of her store, and even a bio
video. She'd double- and triple-checked her online
submission package and then, click, sent it in. That
had been in November, about three months ago.
She'd received the notification that her materials
had successfully arrived but heard nothing else.
Until now.

Emmy looked at her phone again.

Wait. January 23rd. That's today. Today!

Emmy whipped her head around to view the
clock: 12:02. The room spun. The crew would be
arriving in less than two hours.

"Oh, no, no, no!" Emmy moaned. She ran her
hands through her hair and tried to gather her
thoughts. How could this be happening? She
thought about checking the time stamp on the email
to see if she had somehow missed its arrival weeks
before or calling to see if they would reschedule. But
there wasn't time.

"Rachel," Emmy barked into the phone, her
voice a rich baritone. "It's Emmy. This is going to
sound crazy, but tell Jenna to take down all of the
remaining Christmas decorations as fast as

possible. Tell her to put up our February décor. I need you to whip up a batch of Nothing Fancy Fudge. Make it red. We have two hours."

"Emmy? I thought you were sick. What's going on?" Emmy's business partner asked.

"We made it into the competition, Rachel! The Vanderbilt Valentine's Day Candy-Making competition! And they are coming to the store to do an interview at two o'clock."

"Today?"

"Yes! I just got the email. I'll explain more when I get to the store. Just please, hurry!"

"All good, Emmy, you can count on us."

Emmy breathed a sigh of relief. If anyone could pull this off, Rachel could. She could. Together they could.

~

Twenty minutes later Emmy walked into the store a mouth-breathing mess. She had managed to dress in something clean and dry shampoo her hair, but that was about it.

The store, however, looked great. Better than great. It looked incredible.

Maybe they will be so busy admiring the store that they won't focus on me, Emmy thought.

Not only were the last remnants of Christmas completely cleared from the store, but Jenna was in the process of redecorating the tree (oh god, Emmy had completely forgotten about the tree!) with red ribbon and glass heart ornaments.

Emmy started to express her thanks, but Rachel told her there wasn't time. She threw Emmy a bundle of red cloth and told her to sit.

"By some sort of miracle, the shipment of red aprons arrived this morning," Rachel said as she attacked Emmy's hair. She pulled it back into a sleek bun and tied a piece of leftover tree ribbon around it. Then she spun her around and fixed her eye make-up. "There, much better."

Emmy checked her watch: 12:52. They had just about an hour until Pierce and the camera crew were scheduled to show up. Emmy told Jenna to finish up the tree and delegated the kitchen tasks to Rachel. There was no way she was going to serve snot-infested fudge to her guests. It would be safer to stay out of the kitchen altogether, at least until absolutely necessary. Emmy set out table runners and votive candles on the booth tables and then speed-walked through a trial tour, mentally practicing the things she would say.

Their flurry of activity was obvious to any customers who wandered into the store. They refused Emmy's offer of conducting business as usual and promised to stop back later. Besides, that way they could hear all about whatever big to-do was clearly in progress.

At 1:54 Emmy's cold medicine felt like it was working for the first time all day, and at 1:59, Pierce Beaumont arrived at Sweet Shores Chocolate Store.

Chapter 2

"Here we are with Emmy Dawson, our rookie!" Pierce said from beneath a Russian-styled fur hat as Emmy greeted him on the front step of her store.

Oh, Emmy thought. *I guess we are skipping the introductions and going straight to it!*

"Yep, you could say that!" Emmy said and smiled. The red record light of the camera burned a hole in her focus for just a second before she snapped back to attention. "We, ah," she said, faltering for a second, "just celebrated our two-year anniversary this fall. Before that this store was owned and operated for many years by Mr. Edwards. I actually won the store through a Facebook contest!"

"Well, that's certainly an interesting way to begin a business! Maybe later I'll have time to hear all about it," Pierce said.

"Would you like to come inside?" Emmy asked.

"I'd love to. Thank you."

Emmy, Pierce, and the camera crew walked into the store. Emmy smiled at Rachel, who scurried to take his hat and coat.

"This is Rachel Kohl, my business partner," Emmy said.

As Pierce blew right past her, he looked at the camera and said, "Edit that out. No one cares."

As he asked a crew member to fix his hat hair and lint roll his navy suit, Rachel stuck out her tongue at his back, making Emmy stifle a laugh and disguise it as a cough. When Pierce was again deemed camera ready, he turned his attention to the room. Emmy waited in silence for a few seconds as the visitors took in the details of what they saw. Their eyes were drawn immediately to the tree, decorated in gorgeous reds beneath the glowing light of the magnificent chandelier. To the left were the few booths and hot chocolate bar, and to the right the candy counter and kitchens.

"May I make you a cup of hot chocolate before we begin the tour? It does wonders to warm you up and is our signature item here at Sweet Shores Chocolate Store." Emmy guided Pierce over to the hot chocolate bar. It was stocked to bursting with a plethora of delicious ingredients.

Pierce stood before it, looking a bit overwhelmed.

"May I make a suggestion?" Emmy asked graciously.

"Please do," Pierce said.

"To our base of homemade cocoa, I'd recommend adding gingerbread-flavored marshmallows, a drizzle of caramel, and a cinnamon stick to stir it all together."

"I'll take one." When Pierce took his first sip, his frosty demeanor seemed to thaw, just a little.

Cup in hand, he followed Emmy around the store as she talked in nasal tones about her ride through entrepreneurship thus far. Together they scanned the selection of sweets behind the glass counter, while Emmy explained her customers' favorites and the current treat trends in Duluth.

"What have you made for us to taste today?" Pierce asked, abruptly changing the subject. Emmy noticed his cocoa was gone and so was his slightly sweeter disposition.

Emmy was used to seeing his fierce attitude on-screen, but in person Pierce was really quite intimidating. So far, this tour hadn't been as much fun as she thought it would be. A part of her was actually grateful she hadn't had more time to think and prepare for it, because if she had, she knew that she would be disappointed in the host's lack of enthusiasm. She soldiered on.

"Today we've made Nothing Fancy Fudge. It's my business partner's family recipe. It was one of the first items I learned to make for the store," Emmy said and held out a small plated portion for Pierce.

"Because you had never made sweets before, nor gone to school for the culinary arts," Pierce jabbed.

"That's right," Emmy said. "But I've learned a lot in the trenches these past two years and now feel very confident about my skills." She directed his attention back to the treat. "We've dyed the fudge red and used heart-shaped molds for the upcoming Valentine's holiday."

Pierce nodded and took a bite. "Tasty," he said, and nothing more. After a quick tour of the kitchens, Pierce wrapped things up.

"Well, Emmy, thank you for opening your doors and allowing us into your beautiful store. We'll look forward to seeing more from you in North Carolina, at the Vanderbilt Valentine's Day Candy-Making Competition."

"You are welcome! I'm looking forward to it!" Emmy forced herself to be cheerful. Just because Pierce was being a stuffy old prune, didn't mean she needed to follow suit.

"Annnnd, cut." Pierce looked at the camera, and his smile faded.

"Alright, Emmy," Pierce said, extending his hand. "Thank you for your time. Our marketing guy is going to take a few still photos of you here in the store, and then we'll be leaving. I'll see you soon, and remember, life is as sweet as you make it."

Before Emmy could ask any questions, Pierce was out the door and seated in the warm and waiting car just outside.

Chapter 3

When Emmy had graduated from college and started working at the hotel full time, there had been certain things she promised herself that she was going to give up for good. Buying generic toilet paper was one of them. She worked too dang hard to subject her tush to tissue that was abrasive, thank-you-very-much. She was a real grown-up now, and real grown-ups got real toilet paper. Real grown-ups carried umbrellas in their car and always had stamps on hand. Real grown-ups were on time and remembered their friends' birthdays. Real grown-ups drank wine and coffee and had dinner with their boyfriend's parents. Emmy knew all of these things, but at thirty-one she occasionally found herself surprised that she was in fact a grown-up.

As she wheeled her cart around Target, in search of cracked pepper, another bona fide grown-up item, she was lost in thought. What would the other contestants be like? What were they doing to prepare? What specialty items would they know how to make? What would she do with $100,000? This was probably why she turned the corner and ran smack dab into Gloria.

"Oh, my goodness! Gloria! I'm so sorry." Emmy immediately flushed. No matter how many times she saw Gloria, no matter how many times Emmy apologized, and Gloria forgave her... she just couldn't get over the humiliating memory of the first time they met at the Glensheen Mansion. The memory of Gloria's dentures flying across the grand drawing room would permanently be etched into her mind.

"Well, Emmy Dawson!" Gloria said excitedly. "Were your ears ringing this afternoon? Because I was just talking about you!"

Emmy's stomach fluttered. She wasn't 100 percent used to living in a small town yet. Whereas a person could shop, date, live, and breathe almost anonymously in the Twin Cities, it seemed that even the most mundane of life's details were noted and discussed in her new town. Not only that, but one's actions were also open to the critique and interpretation of the others who lived there. Emmy didn't miss the big-city traffic, but she did miss shopping without the contents of her cart being a possible topic of local conversation.

"What about?"

"You, dear! And the TV competition, of course." Gloria beamed. "That lovely Pierce just left Glensheen."

"I didn't know he was still in town," Emmy said, her anxiety starting to rise.

"He is. Or he was. I think he just left," Gloria said and then continued. "Out of the entire board of directors, he picked me to interview! Can you believe it? I told him all about you and your wonderful store and your amazing hot chocolate. I told him about the New Year's Gala and how you were a featured contributor. I even gave him a little tour of the mansion and told him about the history of Duluth. I can't remember the last time I had so much fun or stood next to someone so handsome!"

Emmy nodded as she rambled on. When she took a breath, Emmy cut in.

"Gloria, you didn't, ah, mention the party

pumpkins… and the orange dye… did you?"

Gloria paused and put her finger to her lips. She stayed frozen in thought for several seconds. Emmy fidgeted impatiently.

"You know," Gloria finally said, "I don't remember. It's all kind of a blur now that I look back on it. But I wouldn't worry. That Pierce is such a gentleman. I can't imagine him saying an unkind thing about a single soul. Let alone airing dirty laundry like that on national television."

Emmy nodded. Gloria patted her hand, wished her luck, and continued down the aisle with her cart in the opposite direction.

Emmy stood rooted to the spot in the middle of the frozen food section. Suddenly her cold, which had been held at bay for the last few hours, came back with a raging force. Her head pounded, her eyes watered, and all ability of complex thought, not to mention her grocery list, left her brain. She walked numbly to the checkout and robotically put her items on the conveyor belt, grown-up toilet paper included. She reloaded her cart, paid, and pushed her cart to her car with only one remaining question left lingering in her brain.

What will happen if the mansion story appears on the show? It would be so embarrassing if the whole world knew that the first time she applied to be an event dessert caterer she dyed an entire board of directors' teeth orange. And that when one of the old ladies tried to use water to swish the color away, she accidentally spit her dentures across the room. And then the old woman's friend fainted. Not only did Emmy not get the job, she became the topic of gossip for months.

She hadn't worried about that when she filled out the competition application. But now she realized she should have. She definitely should have considered that possibility. What had she done?

By the time she got home, she was barely functioning. She walked the groceries up to the apartment like a zombie, depositing the bags on the counter, and then just stood there, not knowing what to do next. Numbly she put the food away and made herself a cup of tea. Ignoring Eddie's request to restrict the spread of her germs, she dragged her pillow and comforter from their bedroom and curled up on the couch. She knew she could absolutely do this. She could overcome this devilish disaster from her past, but first, she needed a nap.

~

When Eddie walked in the door at seven, a Stouffer's frozen lasagna was in the oven and Emmy was on the couch. Her laptop balanced on her knees while she took a sip of tea. Eddie tossed his key on the counter, hung up his coat, and walked to the couch. He gently lifted her feet and the mountain of blankets they were piled under and slid beneath them. He looked at her meaningfully and then asked, "How was your day? Feeling better?"

Emmy thought about how to phrase it. "Remember when you took me on the mountain coaster?" Eddie nodded. "It was a lot like that."

"Really?" Eddie asked. He was normally great about staying out of gossip, but Emmy could see from his raised eyebrows that he was intrigued. "Did it have anything to do with that fancy car parked outside your store today?"

"Uh-huh," Emmy said with a huge smile.

The oven timer beeped loudly.

"Okay. I want to hear about it all, the highs and the lows," Eddie said. "But first let me get dinner. Stay put. I'll be back over in a second."

With their dinner spread around them like a living-room picnic, Emmy told Eddie all about her day. From the foggy morning hours to the rush of getting ready, from the thrill of the tour to the worries on her mind, from her restorative nap to the plan she had created in a brand-new document labeled Competition Domination Plan.

"Emmy!" Eddie said when she had finished. "This is amazing! I'm so excited for you."

"I'm sorry I didn't stop into the store to tell you. I tried to, but you were in the middle of an ice cave kayaking demonstration for the Boy Scouts and I didn't want to interrupt."

"No, it's much better this way! What a fun surprise to come home to," Eddie said and then gave her a hug. "It is so much better than the mucous monster I thought I'd be finding when I walked in the door. And my dad will just flip to see Sweet Shores on television."

"We can FaceTime him tomorrow and tell him the good news!" Emmy said and then put down her lasagna plate and curled back up into the covers.

Eddie took the dishes to the kitchen and returned with ice cream. He picked up Emmy's laptop and plugged it in to charge, ignoring her pleas that more work needed to be done. Eddie reached for the remote and queued up several episodes of EatTV's most recent cooking competition.

"This is work," Eddie said, pointing to the TV with a smile. "It's studying. Sort of?"

"Yeah, something like that," Emmy agreed.

Emmy snuggled up to Eddie and put her head on his chest. How did she get so lucky? Every day Eddie made her feel like a champion. As they binge-watched episode after episode, Emmy tried to ignore the sick feeling in her gut... a feeling of nausea that had nothing to do with her horrible head cold. This feeling was grown from the guilt she had about her reason for entering the contest in the first place.

While Pierce Beaumont simultaneously encouraged and scolded contestants on the screen, Emmy battled back and forth as well. She was right. She was wrong. She was justified. She was selfish. Somewhere around midnight in a cloud of exhaustion and cold medicine, she crawled into bed and resolved to figure it all out in the morning.

January 24

Chapter 4

When Emmy's phone rang the next morning, she was elbow deep in a bowl of meringue. Miraculously, she was feeling better. A good night's sleep, plenty of cold medicine, and a healthy dose of adrenaline seemed to have done the trick.

"Alexa, answer phone," Emmy called out and smiled. It had taken her a few weeks to get used to her new virtual assistant, a Christmas gift from Eddie, but now she loved it. Gone were the days of needing to wash her hands every time the phone rang, she wanted to start a new playlist, or she needed to check the weather. Not only was it convenient, it was a major time-saver. Her already chapped hands were also very thankful.

"Well, I think I'm going to change your name from Emmy to contest queen." Emmy smiled as the sound of her mother's voice filled the kitchen. Ever since Emmy had gotten a boyfriend, her relationship with her mother had dramatically improved. Without the tension between them, there was room for so much more... which Emmy and Susan mostly filled with fun.

"It's got a real ring to it, Mom. I'll be sure to ask Pierce Beaumont to address me as Contest Queen at all times." They both laughed.

"When do you leave for North Carolina?" Susan asked.

"How are you so informed?" Emmy asked

incredulously.

"Eddie texted me last night, when you weren't feeling well. He only gave me the basics, but the internet told me everything else. Don't be mad at him. He thought you might want to tell me yourself, but he was worried that I'd hear it from someone else first and be mad."

"No, no, it's fine," Emmy said. "I'm just surprised. I guess good news travels fast."

"It does indeed! So, when do you leave?"

"Next Sunday." Emmy used her well-toned stirring arm to fold in another cup of granulated sugar. "There is a welcome dinner for the contestants that night, and then we start the competition Monday morning."

"And you get to stay at the estate during the filming?" Susan asked, nearly breathless.

"Yep. For as long as I survive in the competition." Emmy began scooping out spoonfuls of meringue in preparation for a batch of Duluth Delites.

"Wow, Emmy, what a dream! Are you ready?"

"Not yet. My list is long."

"Well, then, I'll let you go. Good luck, darling!"

"Thanks, Mom, love you."

"Love you too."

Emmy paused to take a breath and wipe her hands on her apron. Susan's voice was replaced with the smooth sound of Harry Connick Jr.'s crooning. Emmy had put together a playlist of her favorite love songs to inspire her. She'd barely emptied the bowl of meringue before the phone rang again.

"Alexa, answer phone," Emmy said and deposited a load of dirty dishes into the sink.

"Hello, may I speak to Emmy Dawson, please?"

"This is she."

"Hi, Emmy. This is Serena, with the Duluth Young Professionals group. We were wondering if you'd like to speak to our group next Tuesday night. Tell us a little bit about your business and being an entrepreneur and ah…"—here Serena paused—"your upcoming appearance on EatTV?"

"Oh, well, yes," Emmy said as tunnel vision crept at the corners of her eyes. "I'd love to." Emmy's heart beat hard. She stopped moving around her kitchen and closed her eyes. After a short pause Emmy asked, "What time?"

"Amazing. Thank you!" Serena said. "Eleven o'clock. We meet for light lunch at Clyde Iron Works. We'll see you there!"

Emmy heard the click of the line going dead. She leaned up against the refrigerator and slid down it until she sat on the cold kitchen floor.

A flashback from her freshman year in college assaulted her consciousness like a rabid dog.

It was finals week, and for her hospitality management course Emmy was required to present the details of a catering plan to her professor and classmates. As she stood at the front of the lecture hall, she began to sway.

Remembering her roommate's advice, she took a deep breath and bent her knees. But it didn't help. Suddenly she was soaked in sweat. And breathing as if she had run a mile to class instead of walking the three blocks between her apartment and campus.

She had opened her eyes to find her professor's salt-and-pepper-haired head hovering over her, not knowing how she had gotten on the ground or how long she had been laying on the classroom floor. It had been humiliating, and now Emmy had just signed herself up to do it all over again, on live, national television. What was she doing?

How could Emmy have forgotten until this moment that she was petrified of public speaking? She knew the answer and was ashamed to admit it. The honest truth of it was she wanted more than she had. The sickening feelings from last night returned to her gut. Single words pelted her ego like repeated shots from the barrel of a gun. Fame. Success. Attention. Reputation. Status. Prestige.

January 25

Chapter 5

"I've spoken there a bunch of times before," Eddie said as he plunked a casserole-crusted piece of Corningware into a sink full of suds. "It's not that big of a deal."

"It is to me!" Emmy's emotion exploded from her chest and shot across the room at Eddie.

For the first time Emmy could ever remember, Eddie looked hurt. She wanted to take the words back, and yet, she didn't. She meant what she said. It was a big deal to her. They stood across the kitchen from each other, Eddie at the sink and Emmy at the counter, not saying anything.

Emmy broke the silence. "It is a big deal. For me. I know you are super confident in the spotlight, but I'm both nervous and excited and...." Her words trailed off while she thought of something else to say. Finding nothing else to say, she repeated, "It's a big deal to me."

"Okay then," Eddie said. "You better go prepare. Don't worry about the dishes. I've got 'em." He turned his back on her then and stuck his hands into the warm, soapy water.

The argument didn't feel over, but Emmy's angry energy was spent. She didn't know what else she wanted to say anyway, so she walked to the couch and grabbed her laptop. She shoved it into her backpack and then herself into her winter coat, scarf, and hat.

"I'm going to write at Amazing Grace," Emmy

said, and without waiting for a reply or kissing Eddie on the cheek as she always did when they parted, she left.

Emmy hated fighting with Eddie. As she walked across the covered balcony and down the stairs, the argument consumed her mind and made her nauseous. Despite the time Eddie was giving her, she probably wouldn't be able to get any quality work done, and that only fueled Emmy's misery. The fact that these weren't the first cross words they'd said to each other this week didn't help either.

The guilt that had started bubbling in Emmy's stomach the night after the interview with Pierce had grown bigger. She felt equal parts excitement and anxiety about the competition, and at least half of her time was spent wishing she had never signed up in the first place. Maybe a boring existence, free from the stress and anxiety of stardom, would be preferable after all.

She stalked into the cafe just a few minutes later and plopped down into a chair with a noisy sigh.

"Emmy!" Grace said upon seeing her. "What brings you out tonight?"

"I've been invited to speak at the Young Professionals meeting this week, and I have no idea what I'm going to say. I thought maybe a change of scenery would inspire me."

"Oh, I feel you," said Grace, looking at Emmy's dejected expression. "I was so nervous before I spoke to them."

"Really?" Emmy said, already starting to feel a little better. "I was starting to feel pathetic."

"Gosh no," said Grace.

"Well, how did it go? How did you get over your nerves?" Emmy asked, pen poised, ready to take notes.

"I reminded myself that really, I was already doing what they were striving to achieve. I had my own business. I'd kept it open and in the black, and that was something to be proud of. I also reminded myself how much I would have liked some sound advice at their age. I thought about what I wished I would have known before I started. Maybe you can make a list… and go from there." Grace squeezed Emmy on the shoulder and headed back for the kitchen. "You can do it Emmy… you already are!"

"Thanks, Grace," Emmy said.

Emmy sat in the café and thought back to her first few weeks in Duluth. Memories and the smell of baking bread surrounded her. She had been so excited. And so clueless. What advice helped her move forward successfully? What pieces of wisdom saved her? Al and Linda had certainly been helpful. And Eddie. Ugh, Eddie.

Emmy pulled out her phone.

Emmy: I'm sorry I snapped. I'm super stressed and feeling overwhelmed. I didn't mean to take it out on you. I love you.

Emmy waited as the three dots danced on the bottom corner of her screen. When his reply came, Emmy let out the breath she had been holding.

Eddie: I forgive you, of course. And love you always. Even when you are a bit crazy and worry too much. You are going to be a star, Emmy. You can do this!

Renewed by her friend's advice and Eddie's ceaseless faith, Emmy picked up her pen and started making her list, starting with surrounding yourself with supportive family and friends. She also thought back to her very first date with Eddie. Their day-date.

At each location Eddie had taken her, he had tried to teach her a business lesson, specifically about doing business in Duluth. Emmy sucked on her pen cap and let her mind wander back two years.

Their first stop had been to meet Grace, in this very restaurant. While they sat at a table close to this one, Eddie had taught her the first lesson. Good food, good people, and sometimes live music. She'd worked really hard on the first objective and was pretty sure she had succeeded. Her chocolate wasn't award-winning or anything, but it definitely had improved. And the good people part was a no-brainer. Rachel and the rest of her employees were incredible. Her favorite financial guru, Dave Ramsey, advised, "Don't hire crazy and don't hire married to crazy." Emmy's business partner and employees had become more than co-workers. They were now a part of her Duluth family.

At the infamous Glensheen Mansion Eddie had told her, "Never underestimate the power of grandeur and local history." And at Fitger's Brewery Emmy learned that sometimes, to stay afloat, a business needs to be willing to adapt and change with the times. And finally, at Betty's Pies, she was advised to keep her recipes secret.

Those were good pieces of advice. Wisdom that got her through her first year as a store owner… and beyond. These were exactly the kinds of things she should tell the Young Professionals group. Listing her lessons, Emmy realized that they were more than instructions to succeed. Each item on her list—good quality food, great people in her life, the tenacity and drive to be her own boss, and really good recipes—in addition to being a lesson learned, was a blessing.

~

A few nights later Emmy sat in the middle of their bed and tried to explain to Eddie what her stage fright felt like. Her fists were balled up and shoved in the pocket of space between her crisscross flannel-clad legs.

"You know that feeling you get when you've had nothing to drink but caffeinated beverages all day and it's been too long since you last ate?"

"I'd never do that," Eddie said flatly.

"Ugh!" Emmy groaned and threw herself backward onto the bed.

"What? Do you want me to go do it? Chug a bunch of black coffee?"

"Kind of," Emmy said, staring at the ceiling fan blades.

Eddie paused, one hand on the door frame, the other in his back pocket. He shrugged. "Okay." He got two steps down the hall before Emmy called him back, and he lay down next to her on the bed. Emmy laced her fingers in his big calloused ones.

"Tell me instead," Eddie said quietly. Emmy thought about it for a minute. Eddie waited patiently and then gave her hand a squeeze.

"When I have to talk in front of people, large groups especially, my heart beats really fast, like there's not a break in the beats. My hands shake, and the corners of my vision start to go dark. And the worst part is that I can't control it. No matter how many times I tell myself it's no big deal, it still happens. And once it starts, I can't stop it."

"That does sound scary," Eddie said.

"Thanks," Emmy said. "It is. And embarrassing."

The couple lay on the bed for another moment before Eddie leaned up on his elbow and swept Emmy's bangs out of her eyes.

"What if, right before you go on to talk, you envision yourself doing something amazing. Like when you walked into Glensheen and saw your cocoa bar all set up and looking awesome? Or when you made your one thousandth sale and we threw that little party? Or when you graduated from college or we had a great date… or anything that made you feel freaking fantastic? What if you envisioned something like that and let it fill you up? Maybe then there wouldn't be room for the scary."

"You know what, Eddie Edwards," Emmy said as she sat up and looked at him. "You are not only handsome. You are smart and kind, and I love you."

"I love you too," Eddie said. "Now come over here so I can give you something good to think about!" Eddie's arms reached out at laser speed and pulled Emmy to him. Emmy squealed as he began covering her face and neck with bristly bearded kisses.

February 3

On Tuesday afternoon Emmy walked into Clyde Iron Works. The restaurant and bar where the Young Professionals group often liked to meet featured ultra-high ceilings and refurbished industrial windows. Their combination, with exposed brick walls and refurbished wood floors thrown into the mix, was too cool and trendy for the way Emmy was feeling about herself at the moment.

Slightly nauseous, anxious, jittery… broken beer bottles on the floor and sticky barstools might have felt more welcoming, simply for the reason that Emmy knew she could outperform them. But in a room like this? Just being here in the room felt like it elevated her career.

That's what this is all about, remember? Emmy scolded herself. *You are here to do big things. And big things sometimes happen in swanky places.*

Emmy took a deep breath and approached the hostess.

"Hi, I'm Emmy—"

"Dawson," the hostess finished before Emmy could. "I just read about you in the *Tribune*. So great to meet you in person! The rest of the group will be straggling in soon, but Serena is right over there and said to send you in when you arrived."

Emmy smiled and relaxed just a bit. "Thank you."

"Can I send in something to drink for you?" the hostess asked.

"Yes, please, a diet soda would be great."

Emmy crossed the room and tried Eddie's trick of thinking positive. As she walked purposefully across the room, she imagined her feelings of accomplishment when she finally mastered making Duluth Delites. She pictured putting the treats out in the case and selling out before the day was done. She remembered collapsing onto the couch with Eddie that night, both exhausted and elated while they FaceTimed Mr. Edwards to tell him all about it. By the time she stood in front of Serena, she was smiling and actually feeling like she wasn't faking it.

Amid wood-fired flatbread, wings, and bruschetta, Emmy told the gathered members about the lessons she had learned about owning her own business. She talked first about the lessons Eddie taught her directly and then dovetailed into the things she had to figure out herself... sometimes the hard way.

"I'm a dreamer and a doer," Emmy said, "which sometimes works out great! I mean, I moved across the state to run a business that quite literally landed in my lap. Despite knowing nothing about making chocolate, I took a leap and gave it a try. Even though it was free of charge, not everyone would have taken that risk. It worked out for me. But other risks, like trying to cater a dessert for a notoriously distinguished and high-status event just two months in? That one did not work out so great. I guess what I'm saying is... don't be afraid to dream big, but also know that you have to be able to back up those dreams you are shooting for with hard work and a lot of specific knowledge in your field."

The thirty minutes of her presentation flew by. Afterward Emmy answered questions for another thirty minutes. When she went to pick up her business cards, flyers, and coupons from the check table, she found there was nothing left to claim. They were all taken, gone, wanted. Emmy felt great.

"I can see why you like speaking to them," Emmy said to Eddie that night over a dinner of stir-fried vegetables and rice. "It's an adrenaline kick. Like a buzz that lasts for hours. And I wasn't even all that nervous. I mean, I was when I arrived, but then I tried that trick you told me about, you know, envisioning something positive and then, once I started speaking, poof, it was just... great. I wonder if I could go back after the show and talk to them again."

"Uh-oh," Eddie said dramatically. "Looks like I've created a public speaking junkie!"

"You know what?" Emmy asked, chopsticks poised in the air. "I don't even care that you are making fun of me right now because I have just overcome my stage fright."

February 7

Chapter 6

Emmy was completely shocked when her mother walked through the front door of her store at ten o'clock Saturday morning. Emmy rushed to hug her and then happily asked, "What are you doing here?"

"I've come to take out my girl! Shopping, nails, lunch! We need to get you ready!" Susan said cheerily.

Emmy's face fell. "I can't. We have so much to do!" She turned to look at Rachel and the to-do list they had just been revising.

"We've got you covered. Both Jenna and Samantha are on their way in. Your mom called yesterday to see if she could come and treat you before you head to the show."

"And you said yes?!?!" Emmy said, pointing to the lengthy list on the counter. "We have sooooo much to do."

"Don't worry about it. We'll be fine."

"We are going to be late if you don't hustle," Susan said. Her look, one refined from years of motherhood, gave Emmy very little room for arguing.

"Give me just a second," Emmy said to her mom and squeezed her in a hug again.

"I'll be in the car. Warming it up. Good lord it's cold here," Susan said as she walked toward the exit.

Emmy joined her two minutes later, smiling

giddily in a way she hadn't for a long time.

"Where first?" she asked, rubbing her gloved hands on her thighs to warm them.

"Hair. You need a fresh cut before going on national television. And some color too. And your eyebrows could use some waxing."

"Ahh, thank you?" Emmy laughed. Susan pulled away from the curb and drove from Canal Park toward the center of the city.

"And then we're getting our nails done. Those cooking shows always zoom in for close-ups of the bakers' hands, and we do not want your cuticles in their current state getting any airtime." Emmy rolled her eyes at her sixty-year-old mother's assessment of her personal style but reasoned she was probably right. Either way, Emmy knew it would do no good to argue. "Then we'll shop until it's time to meet Eddie and your father at the Boat Club for dinner."

"Dad's here too?" Emmy asked.

"Of course. He didn't want to miss it," Susan said and checked her blind spot before switching lanes. "He and Eddie are spending the day gathering all of the supplies your father will need for several silent auction baskets for his company's annual gala. I don't think it will take all day. Eddie mentioned something about a brewery tour or something, so I'm not worried about how they'll occupy their time. I did warn them, however, not to show up to dinner in poor form, if you know what I mean."

"You guys are the best!" Emmy said, thrilled at their thoughtfulness. "Thank you."

"Yes, yes of course," Susan swatted away her sentimentality with a gloved hand. "Now, tell me how to get to London Road so we can go to Vain Salon. I'm lost."

~

When Emmy walked through the doors of the Duluth Boat Club toward Eddie and her father, already waiting at their reserved table, she felt like a million bucks. And she should. She and her mother had spent a small fortune today. Emmy tried to pay, repeatedly, but her mother refused her card, her cash, and her offers to pay her back.

"How often does one's daughter go on national television?" Susan asked.

"You keep saying national television like it's a Nobel prize," Emmy said and rolled her eyes.

"Well, it's a big deal, Emmy! And I just want you to look and feel your best for it," Susan said with puppy-dog eyes and an honest to goodness pout. Emmy swatted her with a bag from Pichardo Boutique, causing her mother to crack a smile. "Just let me do this for you?"

"Okay," Emmy said, returning her smile. "If I have to!"

"Good. Now, let's get down to business. You'll need a dress for dinner. The banquet hall at the Biltmore is fit for a queen. You'll want something nice in case they do a fancy dinner. Plus, you can give it a trial run tonight."

As Emmy walked to the table that night, she knew she and her mother had selected a winner. The dress moved with her effortlessly, and Eddie's expression was a true indication of success. His smile reached all the way up to his green eyes.

"Well, it looks like you ladies have had a productive day!" he said and kissed her on the cheek before pulling out her chair.

"We had a marvelous time," Susan said, sliding into her own chair, held out by her husband.

"We really did," Emmy agreed. "Hair, nails, lunch, shopping. I've been properly spoiled all day long."

The server arrived then. After taking their drink order and delivering it, he took their food order and promptly disappeared. After their first sips—wine for the women, whiskey for the men—the foursome relaxed into their plush chairs and settled into comfortable conversation.

"So, tell us about the show, Emmy," her dad said.

For two solid hours Emmy rambled on about EatTV and their prior shows and contestants and the prize packages and success stories. Eddie and her parents oohed and aahed. They smiled and nodded and let Emmy jabber the night away. Several hours later she and Eddie waved goodbye to Emmy's parents from their balcony and watched them drive away.

"What a great day," Emmy said.

"I'm so glad you thought so," Eddie said. As Emmy tried to stand on one foot and remove her strappy shoe from the other, Eddie pulled her backwards onto the bed. She toppled onto him with a playful shriek. Eddie waded through the pools of dress fabric to find her face and kiss her. When he broke away from her lips he said, "I have a parting gift."

"That wasn't necessary!" Emmy said as she

scooted up to lean back against the pillows.

"I know," said Eddie as he leaned on one elbow and reached inside his suit coat. "That's what makes it fun." He removed a small box and held it out to Emmy. He looked at Emmy meaningfully and then opened the black velvet box.

Inside was a delicate silver chain. Dangling from the center was a miniature teaspoon. The charm was made of silver as well, but in the center of the spoon was a heart-shaped ruby. Emmy clutched the box to her heart.

"I love it!" she said and kissed him. "Thank you!" Emmy thrust the box back into Eddie's hand and spun around so he could fasten the necklace around her neck.

"Now, no matter where you are," Eddie said, turning her around again, "if you ever get nervous, just give the heart a little rub and you can know that I'm sending you spoonfuls of luck and love."

February 8

Chapter 7

Emmy walked through the automatic doors of the airport with a vise grip on Eddie's hand. Eddie took one look at her pale face and pulled her out of the flow of foot traffic. As they stood in front of a gift shop, Emmy's eyes filled with tears. Through her glassy vision she saw t-shirts and coffee mugs professing their love of Minnesota.

"Hey," Eddie said gently. "Look at me."

Emmy shook her head to communicate a tiny no.

"Listen," Eddie said, lifting her chin. "You don't have to do this. Sweet Shores will be just fine without the added publicity. If you want to go back home and watch the show from the couch, I won't love you less. Even if the store somehow closed for good, you'd still be my favorite chocolatier."

Emmy rolled her eyes, causing tears to spill down her cheeks.

"What if I wanted to run the lift bridge instead? Or be a yoga master or join the circus?" she asked.

"Even if you decided that your heart was calling you to work for the City of Duluth Sanitation Department... I would still love you." He wrapped Emmy in a hug. "I just might ask you to shower a bit more often. And I'd miss the sweet, sugary way your hair always smells when you come home."

Emmy took a deep breath. Eddie stood patiently, holding her hand, steady as a lighthouse.

"It feels guilty to say this, but I want more. It's not that I want to be famous. Or maybe I do. I don't know. I just want to do more than survive. I know that if the store crashed and burned that you could support me, support us. I just…" Emmy sighed. "I want my business to be more than just fine." She spat the last word out as if it were venom.

Emmy felt her stomach roll and knew she wasn't telling the whole truth. Eddie opened his mouth to console her, but she cut him off.

"It's not like I want to compete with you… I guess I'm just a little… jealous."

"Jealous?" Eddie raised his eyebrows. "Is that what all this tension between us has been about?" Eddie asked in sudden realization.

"Yes! Jealous!" Emmy laughed at his inability to see his own good fortune and wiped the tears neatly from beneath her eyes. "Everyone knows you. You're the hometown hero hockey player whose store is super successful. I'm just that girl that dates Eddie."

"Stop," Eddie said seriously. "You are more than that. So much more. Come on, Emmy."

"I'm just saying that sometimes it feels that way. It would be nice to be recognized for my own efforts and achievements. And as scared as I am to go on TV, I think this competition might be my golden ticket."

Eddie looked at her and Emmy looked back, appraising the effects of their full honesty.

"It will be hard to win if you miss your flight," Eddie finally said.

"Thank you for understanding," Emmy said. "And for loving me always."

"There was never any doubt about that. Now get going."

Emmy hoisted her carry-on bag up onto her shoulder and then gave Eddie a long goodbye kiss. As she wound through the maze of security, she realized she felt better already. Without the burden of her negative feelings, everything felt lighter, except her backpack, which was stuffed to the gills. She could do this. Just one thing at a time, and right now, the thing that needed to be done was getting on a plane.

~

Once they were up in the air and the adrenaline rush of takeoff subsided, Emmy pulled out the packet from EatTV that had come in the mail last week. When it arrived, she filled out and mailed back the necessary paperwork: the insurance form, the confidentiality agreement, and the contestant questionnaire. As tempting as the rest of the competition information was, Emmy was too busy preparing to leave.

In the short time between receiving the acceptance email and leaving for North Carolina, she had prepared the store for her absence. She wanted to leave Rachel and the store in a good spot. A dozen batches of fudge, three trays of Duluth Delites, and oodles of individually wrapped caramels were made and ready for sale. The hot cocoa bar was fully stocked, including the back-up canisters, so that if one ingredient ran out, another was all set to go. Emmy had also assembled a TV-worthy wardrobe and done some social media promotion, not to mention speaking at the Young Professionals group and her wonderful day date with her mother. She'd done everything she could to be ready… for both events happening in Minnesota and North Carolina.

Emmy turned her attention back to her lap and the awaiting competition information. From the large envelope Emmy pulled a black dossier. On the front of the glossy cover, red metallic letters emblazoned the words: Vanderbilt Valentine's Day Candy-Making Competition. Emmy opened up the dossier and found a one-page profile for each contestant. Her body reacted in excitement and dread simultaneously. With her gut clenching and her heart racing, she began to study up on her competition.

Emmy assumed they were arranged alphabetically, because Silvia Alvarez was first.

For more than three decades Silvia Alvarez, "the creative confectioner," has been dazzling the state of Texas with both her art and her scrumptious candy. Silvia sells her delectable creations to several boutique candy stores and ice cream parlors around the state and is known for her gorgeous sweets that look almost too good to eat. From this competition Silvia is hoping to take her work to a national stage. If she wins the competition, she plans to create a taste and see museum with edible art installments for people of all ages. Her cookbook will showcase images and recipes for the museum's delicious displays.

Emmy turned the page.

Otis Anderson, "the eco-candy creator," believes that only the best natural ingredients are meant to be ingested. He infuses his green and sustainable lifestyle into every treat he makes. Hailing from Portland, it's no surprise that this hipster turned candy maker is a big mover and shaker in the natural-foods world. If given the prize money, Otis says he will use it to start a greenhouse for ingredients in his new line of products called Green Space Sweets. Otis's cookbooks will include organic recipes for candy makers of all ages. He commits that a portion of the proceeds will be given to environmental organizations.

When Emmy flipped to the next page, a gorgeous blonde, the epitome of a Southern belle, smiled back at her. How did she get her eyes to sparkle like that? Emmy wondered. Emmy was shell-shocked by her beauty. Could this woman possibly be as talented as she was pretty? Emmy read on.

Callie Ann Collins, "the hometown hero," has been the sweetheart of Asheville her entire life. Being the granddaughter of long-time mayor Beau Collins has made her a staple of Asheville's society life since she was old enough to smile for the camera. The town has always loved her, but recently, they have become obsessed with her ingenious twists on classic sweets. Her treats, sold at charity fundraisers and served at state dinners, have been getting rave reviews. With her prize money Callie Ann will create a line of designer aprons and kitchen accessories. Her cookbook, tentatively titled *Cooking Couture*, will feature not only her sweets, but showcase these fashions.

Emmy tore her eyes away from Callie Ann's dazzling smile and found her own face on the next page.

"Hey, that's you," said the woman in the seat next to her.

"Oh," said Emmy, startled. "Yes, yes, it is." She slid the black folder over to the woman. "I'm too nervous to see what they wrote about me. Can you read it, please?"

The woman nodded and then started to read aloud.

"Emmy Dawson, "the rookie," is new to the candy-making world. She took over the day-to-day operations of a small chocolate store in Duluth, Minnesota, with no prior training in either business or candy making. Surpassing all odds, her little store is surviving. Customers claim her signature hot cocoa bar is one of the town's winter must-visit destinations. With the prize money Emmy reported that she would open a new store location on her town's ski hill, Spirit Mountain, and serve her delicious cocoa to all the shredders and ski bunnies. Her cookbook plans are to make a Sweet Shores collective memoir, in which several Lake Superior legends share a recipe and a piece of their life.

Emmy let out a breath. It wasn't awful, but the word choice wasn't exactly inspiring confidence.

"I think it sounds like a lovely idea," the woman said. "I'd read that book."

"Thank you," Emmy said and smiled at the sweet woman. "You can watch the competition this week on EatTV, and if I win, I'll send you a copy. Here, write down your address." Emmy opened the back of the dossier and handed the woman a pen. The woman wrote her name and address and then handed the folder and pen back to Emmy.

"I'd love to chat more, but I have to study up," Emmy told the woman. "I only have four hours on this flight to read through this and memorize about a dozen recipes."

"Go, go. Don't let me distract you." The woman waved Emmy off and smiled. She opened up her *HGTV* magazine and disappeared behind its glossy cover.

Emmy returned to her competitors.

Jean Luc Martin, "the lovable Frenchman," grew up baking pastries in his grandfather's kitchen on the outskirts of Paris. When he was a teen he struck out on his own, traveling the countryside learning all that he could from chefs and bakers and chocolatiers. His lifetime of experience and generous heart, not to mention his several international awards, make him another contest favorite. Jean Luc plans to use his contest winnings to open a bed and breakfast in the French countryside and spend the rest of his years hosting and feeding those who visit. His cookbook will feature desserts and pastries with a French flair.

Oh goodie, another pro. Emmy sighed.

Andy Morrison, "the candy connoisseur," claims he eats as much candy as he makes... and that's saying something. His specialty? Cotton candy. He has been stocking his hometown of Nashville with this sweet treat for the past five years. Cotton Candy Andy, as locals call him, bounces around town on a constant sugar high, creating and selling hundreds of flavors of fluffy, flavorful cotton candy. Andy's cookbook will teach young cooks how to make their own cotton candy at home and some of the science behind cooking as well. The prize money? Andy has yet to decide how he would spend his winnings, but he says a traveling hot air balloon store is currently topping the list.

Marguerite Pearl, "the grand duchess of desserts," graduated at the top of her class from the London School of Culinary Confections and has put her expert skills to use in five-star resorts across the continent of Europe. It is rumored that the Queen of England requested Marguerite's sweets to fill the eggs at last year's Buckingham Palace Easter egg hunt. Her specialty item is malted milk covered in fine chocolate and topped with complementary flavor stripes. The citrus zest (with real fruit!) variety is a national best seller in her home country of England. With her prize winnings, Marguerite plans to open a culinary school of her own. Her cookbook contract will be used to create a practical application textbook for future students.

Gerard Taylor, "the familiar face," has been filling truffles for the past two decades. We know, because we've watched him do it—and so have you! Gerard was formerly the actor on the Lindt truffle commercials. In a surprise move, this veteran chocolatier has decided to extend his screen time by joining the Vanderbilt Valentine's Day Candy-Making Competition. Not surprisingly, Gerard's cookbook would feature truffles. He plans to use his prize money to open his own start-up chocolate company. It should be noted that Gerard is in the competition representing himself as an individual entity, and not Lindt Chocolate, his former employer.

Well at least my introduction wasn't as bad as all that, Emmy thought.

It didn't take much reading between the lines to see there was a whole lot of drama surrounding Gerard. Emmy looked carefully at his smiling profile picture, his eyebrow arching up to touch the brim of his baker's hat, and wondered what was going on in his head.

Emmy put down the dossier and rummaged in her backpack for a snack. She thought about pulling out her recipe cards to do a little studying, but after reading through her competitors' rap sheets, she needed a little fortification. Instead, she grabbed a little baggie of pretzel poppers, a creation she had concocted this summer. Bite-sized pretzel pieces were drizzled with stripes of caramel— Emmy's favorite ingredient—and then dusted with milk chocolate powder. It was the perfect combination of sweet and salty. She reached further into her backpack and produced another bag of the treats and offered them to the woman next to her.

"I made them myself," Emmy said as the woman examined the Sweet Shores Chocolate Store seal on the bag.

"Thank you," said the woman. "All I've had today is airport coffee and a stale bagel from the hotel continental breakfast."

As they chatted Emmy got the strange feeling that she had met this woman before. She looked so familiar. But Emmy hadn't left Duluth in months, and this woman never said a thing about visiting the North Shore, so Emmy let it go. She must just look like someone Emmy knew.

They talked mostly about family. The woman had three children, the middle of which was dramatically pining for a girl in his biology class. The

Valentine's Day dance was fast approaching, and the power was entirely out of his hands. As was tradition in his school, the dance during this time of year was Sadie Hawkins Style... the girls asked the boys, and not the other way around.

"He's spent the last week moping because she picked Ross Granderson to be her partner for the cell project. My son swears his life is over!" The two women chuckled.

"Well here," Emmy said as she reached into her backpack and handed over a bag of sweets. Rachel had suggested she bring extras to hand out to people she met or to leave randomly in the hotel lobby. Free advertising, she called it. Emmy was glad she listened. "Give him one of these. He can leave it in her locker with a sweet note. Maybe it will win him some points."

The woman took the bag of red heart juju candies and smiled. "Thank you so much. And best of luck in the competition. I won't bore you with the details, but I've been in your shoes. Stay true to your sweet and generous self, and you'll be fantastic."

"Thank you," Emmy paused. "You know, we've been talking this entire flight and I didn't even ask your name."

They were standing up now, the illumination of the seat-belt release sign a shotgun start to begin exiting the place. Emmy sidestepped into the aisle and shouldered her carry-on, doing her best not to bump into the other passengers. The woman stepped into the aisle and stuck out her hand.

"I'm Amelia. Amelia Grace." Her new passenger friend winked and then smiled broadly as

Emmy's eyes widened in recognition. "Life is as sweet as you make it, Emmy. I hope yours will be a treat to remember."

With that final parting phrase, Amelia left Emmy starstruck and dumbstruck, causing a disgruntled traffic jam to bog up behind her.

Amelia Grace. First ever winner of an EatTV cooking competition. The Kelly Clarkson of the cooking world. Sitting right next to her. Talking to her! Wishing her luck!! Was this a good omen? Emmy wondered. Five minutes after departing the plane, she wasn't so sure.

Chapter 8

Her plane arrived late, her suitcase was nowhere to be found, and the driver who was supposed to be picking her up in front of the car rental kiosk was nowhere in sight. When Emmy realized that her watch was still on Minnesota time, an hour earlier than the current time in Asheville, North Carolina, she almost lost her mind right there on the airport faux marble floor.

A string of curse words flew through her mind as she frantically looked for an exit sign. Spotting a set of sliding automatic doors, Emmy launched herself in their direction and out into the North Carolina afternoon. It wasn't as warm as she thought it would be, but at least she didn't turn into a human popsicle the second she stepped outside.

At the first sign of a yellow car, she threw her hand in the air like a seasoned New Yorker and shouted, "Taxi!"

Miraculously, the woman behind the wheel pulled to the curb immediately and allowed Emmy to hop in.

"Where to, hunnie?" the gum-snapping cabbie drawled.

"Biltmore Estates, please."

"Well, you sure picked the fanciest place in town!"

"Is it far?" Emmy asked.

"Just about twenty minutes," the cabbie said before checking her rearview mirror and pulling into the outgoing airport traffic.

"Thank you," Emmy said. "I'm going to be on a reality TV show that is being filmed at the estate.

I'm running late and the airline lost my luggage, so I'm feeling a little frazzled."

"Well, you just sit back, relax, and let Ruby get you there."

Emmy tried to follow orders, but it was difficult. Before she could get herself worked into an anxiety attack, Emmy leaned back in her seat and closed her eyes. She felt a bit guilty about missing the scenery, but a quiet moment was what she needed to pull herself together. As she absentmindedly rubbed the charm on her necklace from Eddie, she replayed the wonderful events of yesterday in her mind. Again, the trick worked. Knowing that her parents and Eddie supported her, no matter what, definitely helped too.

True to her word, Ruby pulled onto the Vanderbilt property exactly twenty minutes later.

The cab drove beneath a brick archway and started down the long winding road. They passed densely growing trees, and beneath their branches Emmy spotted a bridge traversing a small creek. On either side of the one-way driveway, a beautifully manicured lawn laid out in resplendent glory. Emmy imagined that in the summer it would look even more amazing, but even now it was impressive. Across the lawn, directly to her left, Emmy caught a glimpse of an identical road stretching in the opposite direction. She hoped that she would not find herself on it too soon, driving away before she was ready to leave.

Between the two roads, in the very center of the rectangular lawn, was a circular pond. In the center of it, a fountain sent streams of water in all directions, creating concentric ripples that lapped against the stone rim of the pool. As beautiful as it was, Emmy's attention was quickly diverted. Through the windshield, the mansion came into view. On the drive, Ruby had proudly told her that it was the largest privately-owned home in the nation, but that description didn't begin to do it justice.

Magnificent. Splendid. Grand. Descriptors shot through Emmy's brain rapid-fire, like the Bayfront Festival Fourth of July fireworks. She felt her jaw drop and her eyes go wide. Ruby's voice brought her back to the present.

"What's goin' on up here?"

Emmy directed her gaze to the crowd gathered in front of the steps leading into the house. Among the crowd were several people standing behind large cameras. Emmy's sense of wonder crashed to the car mats beneath her feet. She leaned forward and checked her reflection in Ruby's rearview mirror. It didn't really matter what she saw in the reflection; there was nothing she could do about it now. Emmy looked down at her wardrobe and was relieved to see that she'd chosen something at least slightly stylish. She was wearing leggings, boots, and an oversized sweater, attire that was dually comfortable for air travel and warm enough for her to leave her coat in Eddie's truck.

When Ruby slowed to a stop, Emmy handed her a wad of bills and told her to keep the change.

"Here goes nothing," she muttered to herself.

"Go on, be a star!" Ruby encouraged. "What's the point if you don't have a little fun?"

Emmy thought of the text Eddie had sent her about a week ago giving the same advice. *You are going to be a star.*

"Amen, Ruby," Emmy said and then grabbed her backpack and pulled on the door handle.

Emmy stepped out of the car and turned on what she hoped was a confident smile. Since her luggage was decidedly lost, there was nothing for her to grab from the trunk, so she gave the roof of the car a double tap, like she'd seen big-city people do in the movies, and then walked toward the awaiting camera crew.

Pierce was there to greet her.

"Last to arrive is Emmy Dawson!" he said congenially to the cameras. "Emmy, welcome to The Biltmore."

"Thank you, Pierce! I'm glad to be here," Emmy said, offering him her hand to shake. "It's nice to see you again."

"Indeed. Tell us quick, just how far do you aspire to go in this competition?"

"My dad always says, go big or go home," Emmy said with a little laugh. "So, I'm in for the long haul, I guess!"

"Are you intimidated by the lineup of contestants?" Pierce leaned in closer with his microphone. He winced too, making the question seem almost painful to ask.

Wow, nothing like going for the jugular, Emmy thought.

"Maybe a little?" Emmy said and pinched her pointer finger and thumb together. She hoped the action came off as a bit funny and totally relatable. "Honestly, who wouldn't be? All of the contestants here have amazing resumes. Really, I'm just honored to be included in the lineup. I'm excited to meet everyone and hopefully learn a few new tricks as well."

"I like your approach," Pierce said with a thoughtful nod. "Best of luck to you, Emmy Dawson. And remember, life is as sweet as you make it!"

After Pierce said the contest tagline, he dropped the microphone and Emmy saw the red lights on the cameras extinguish. She tipped her head back and looked at the tan and green spires of the mansion reaching to the sky. Then she dropped her gaze a foot or so at a time, taking in the intricate stonework and innumerable windows. When she finally looked back at Pierce, he was massaging his jaw and looking at her. Apparently, it was a lot of work to arrange your facial muscles just so.

"Whenever you are ready, you can head on in," Pierce said warmly. "The other contestants have already arrived and are taking a little personal time in their rooms. We will meet for dinner at six and then watch the first episode together in the drawing room. Afterward, Dixie will go through a few contest regulations and rules, and then we'll turn you loose to bed."

Emmy smiled at him. "Thank you. It's been kind of a hectic day. My plane arrived late and the airline lost my luggage." Emmy shrugged and then let out a big sigh. "But I'm here now."

"We're glad you are. Go on up the steps; someone will be waiting there to show you to your room."

As Emmy walked up the steps, she wondered if she had somehow misremembered Pierce. He seemed so kind and warm just now. Had it been her head cold that had cast him in such a severe light before? Before she could decide, an estate employee was greeting her.

Ready or not, Emmy thought, *here we go.*

Chapter 9

The marble staircase wrapped around the room like a gigantic serpent, an elegant white beast with intricate black railings and red velvet rope adornments. Several circular chandeliers lit with cream-colored candles hung intermittently between the floor and ceiling, marking the number of floors a person would traverse from top to bottom, or the other way around. Just like the Glensheen Mansion, Emmy found this place to be magic. Even her thoughts were prettier here. She wasn't a writer by trade, but as she tried to describe the Biltmore in her head, so she could remember and tell her mother and friends later, she found her internal thoughts had a flow and elegance she usually lacked in her regular day-to-day life. She hoped that this sudden way with words would follow her onto the TV screen.

Emmy entered the grand banquet hall five minutes ahead of schedule to find the other contestants already mingling near one of the three massive fireplace grates. With champagne in hand and clothes that were obviously not travel weary, they looked downright glamorous. Emmy took a deep breath and went to join them. On the walk down, she had decided to approach Silvia first. Her picture, a big smile on her face, looked the friendliest.

A waiter handed Emmy a flute of bubbling golden liquid. Emmy took a sip and then walked up to Silvia, who was laughing at something Jean Luc had said.

"Hello! I'm Emmy Dawson," she said and

stuck out her hand.

"Emmy, hello, lovely to meet you," Silvia said and squeezed her hand. "Jean Luc was just telling me the funniest story. Go on Jean Luc, tell it again."

Jean Luc shook Emmy's hand, took a sip of his champagne, and then repeated his story. It really was funny. When he was a boy, he had worked in his grandfather's pastry shop and one day misplaced the key to the cupboard where the expensive spices and ingredients were kept. Saffron. Truffles. Vanilla. Cardamom. Cloves. He and his grandfather had looked for the key all day, with no luck. But when they sat down for dinner, and Jean Luc bit into his roll, he found it.

"It gave a whole new meaning to the phrase 'by the skin of my teeth!'" Jean Luc said and laughed. "Had I not found that key, my grandfather surely would have taken it out on my hide!"

Emmy laughed along with them. Between their friendliness and the champagne, she was feeling much better. Maybe she had been worrying for nothing. Just then Dixie walked into the room and the happy chatter of the contestants died down.

"Please, take your seats," she said and then moved to the head of the table.

Even though a large table made up most of the room, the contestants, along with Dixie and Pierce, sat at a smaller, more intimate table in front of the fireplace. Emmy found the seat with her name placard and sat down. She was disappointed to see that Silvia and Jean Luc were seated the furthest from her. She turned to her left and saw Marguerite Pearl, and to her right, Callie Ann Collins.

Emmy tried to eat her salad as delicately as

possible and suddenly wished her mother had forced her to take etiquette lessons as a teen. Which fork exactly was she supposed to use? Just as she popped a bite of spinach and arugula into her mouth, Callie Ann spoke up.

"Dixie, do you mind if we play a quick dinner party game? It'll help us get to know one another a little better." She smiled sweetly in the direction of the producer.

"Of course," Dixie said, lifting her champagne toward Callie Ann. "What a lovely idea."

"Alright. Here's how it works. I'll come up with a question, and then one at a time we will each share our answer."

Emmy's stomach gave a little lurch. She had a sudden flashback to her days of slumber parties and the infinite horrors that emerged when playing truth or dare.

Callie Ann rolled her eyes heavenward and put her finger to her lips as she appeared to think of a good question. "Oh, I know. What was your favorite childhood candy, and what is your favorite now?"

Emmy breathed a subtle sigh of relief. This she could do.

"Ooh! Good question!" Silvia beamed. "Who wants to go first?"

"I will," Otis said, wiping his mouth with his cloth napkin.

Callie Ann, seated at Otis's left elbow, looked a little put out that her stage had been stolen, but nodded in his direction and said, "Otis, why don't you go first?" like it had been her idea all along.

"We'll go around the table and end with me." She nodded again as if to convince herself, and everyone else at the table, that this was a good idea.

"Okay," Otis started. "Well, as a child my favorite candy was root beer barrels, but now as an adult I prefer slightly salted seaweed treats."

"Eww!" said Emmy before she caught herself.

"Emmy, don't be rude!" Callie Ann scolded.

"I'm sorry, I was just taken by surprise," Emmy said, her cheeks flushing. "I mean, really, Otis? Seaweed?"

"It's delicious," he said with a sniff.

"Well, everybody gets to pick!" Emmy said and then worked to move the conversation along. "Dixie, what are your favorites?"

"As a child I loved saltwater taffy, but now... good lord, I can't remember the last time I ate a piece of candy. I guess I'll just have to pass on that one."

Emmy looked at the prim, probably size two, producer and thought she was most likely telling the truth.

"How sad for you," Silvia said and leaned over to pat her hand in sympathy. "I eat candy every day. My favorites as a kid were juju candies... you know those little fruit-flavored ones? I could eat them by the pound! And now, my favorite is a good chocolate-covered cherry. Not those ones from a box! The homemade kind."

Gerard and Jean Luc shared as well, listing truffles and peppermint patties as their current favorites and Hershey Kisses and licorice as the fixes for their younger selves' sweet tooth. Andy said that he always had, and always will, love cotton candy. Pierce had to be cajoled into participating, but finally admitted that as a boy he loved Charleston Chews and as a grown up savored Raisinets, especially at the movie theater. Emmy imagined the pristinely proper host taking a huge bite out of a chocolate-covered mallow bar—a string of the gooey sugars strung across his chin—and smiled.

Marguerite shared that she used to love malted milk balls; everyone in England did. But now, when she wanted to indulge, she chose only the finest dark chocolate. Her favorite was from Switzerland.

"As a little girl I loved Smarties," Emmy said. "But now caramel is my favorite. Anything with caramel. In fact, it's kind of funny, but when I first opened my chocolate store, I didn't even like chocolate, I—"

"Well, my favorite," Callie Ann said, cutting off Emmy, "are chocolate-covered coffee beans. I'm telling you, it's the sweetest caffeine buzz you'll ever experience. And when I was a little girl, I loved jelly beans, especially the orange ones."

From there the conversation dissolved into pockets of chitchat around the table. Emmy enjoyed her meal but found it difficult to join in the discussions. No matter what she said, Marguerite seemed to snub her, and Callie Ann seemed to not even hear her comments because she kept talking over her. Finally, Emmy resigned to simply listen. She watched the interactions of the other contestants and gauged their reactions to one another. Even though it wasn't typically in her nature to sit back passively, she learned a lot about her competition and at the end of the meal, considered it a success.

After dinner the contestants gathered in the drawing room to watch the first episode together. Even though they had done very little filming since arriving, the footage shot in the contestants' hometowns was enough to constitute an hour's worth of prime-time television. The once chatty group now sat in nervous silence. Only Dixie still fluttered about the room, running a constant commentary. As the TV screen showed an aerial view of the estate and the familiar theme song filled the room, Marguerite actually shushed her. Despite her nerves, Emmy smiled.

Over the backdrop of the mansion's manicured lawns, a cookbook appeared and magically flipped opened. A spritz of glitter sporadically sparkled from the screen each time the pages turned and revealed the smiling face of another contestant. When all the competitors had been shown, the cookbook disappeared and the camera flew across the lawn, through the front doors and throughout the house, giving viewers a super-speed tour before bursting through the kitchen doors and coming to a rest on the handsome figure of Pierce Beaumont. The music faded, and Pierce took over.

"Good evening, and welcome to the historic home of the Vanderbilts. This season EatTV will be bringing you another heated cooking competition from the kitchen of The Biltmore Estates. Here, eight talented candy makers will compete to outdo one another, impress the judges, and win your hearts. Their prize for doing so? This season it's bigger than ever! In addition to $100,000, the best candy maker will also win a traditional cookbook deal, so the entire country can enjoy the goodness of their creations from the comfort of their own homes. Can you imagine anything more delicious? We always tell our contestants that life is as sweet as they make it, but now you can join in the fun too."

Pierce walked from the kitchen to a nearby room decorated in what could only be described as opulent style.

"Before we go any further," he said, sitting down in a high-backed chair made of mahogany and upholstered in purple and gold velvet, "let's meet our contestants!"

Starting with Silvia, just as the dossier had done, the screen showed the contestants' hometown interviews. Emmy noted her competitors' different reactions to seeing themselves on-screen. Silvia sat up a bit straighter. Jean Luc bit the knuckle of his thumb. Otis stroked the very tip of his beard. Callie Ann actually emitted a tiny squeal and visibly bounced on the edge of her velvet-clad seat. Marguerite clasped her hands together tightly and pursed her lips. When Andy first saw his face on the screen, he rapidly and quietly clapped his hands together to dispel his nervous energy. Only Gerard's face was a blank canvas, the excitement of seeing himself on TV long since spent.

Interesting facts about each candy maker's style and workplace floated around Emmy in a sugary haze as she anticipated her own time slot. After Callie Ann it was her turn. Emmy cursed inside and wondered at the unfairness of having to trail the walking, talking, baker Barbie.

When her head-cold face filled the screen next, her stomach sank. Had her nose really been that red? Her eyes that watery? The footage started with Emmy and Pierce just outside Sweet Shores Chocolate Store. The desolate winter streets were bare, and the lake was barely distinguishable amidst the white of the snow and the fog in the air. On-screen Emmy sniffed and shivered.

"Here we are with Emmy Dawson, our rookie!" Pierce said from beneath a Russian-styled fur hat. Somehow, he didn't look cold at all.

"Yep, you could say that!" Emmy said and smiled. "We just celebrated our two-year anniversary this fall. Before that this store was owned and operated for many years by Mr. Edwards. I actually won the store through a Facebook contest!"

"Well, that's certainly an interesting way to begin a business!" Pierce said with a knowing look in the camera.

"Would you like to come inside?" Emmy asked the smug Pierce.

"I'd love to. Thank you."

As Emmy, Pierce, and the camera crew walked into the store, the film angle dropped back from the close-up it had been holding on Emmy's sinus-suffering profile and took in the entire store.

In real time Emmy heard Jean Luc let out a low whistle and Callie Ann say, "Wow." Her store really was impressive. Her hopes that it would take center stage were fulfilled. For the next few minutes, Pierce followed Emmy around the store as she talked in nasal tones about her ride through entrepreneurship thus far. They scanned the selection of sweets behind the glass counter, toured the kitchen, and tasted the sample fudge, which Pierce declared "tasty" and nothing more. Up until that point, the moments they chose to display in the episode were fine. Just fine.

When Emmy saw Gloria's face fill the screen, she broke out in a cold sweat.

Please, she begged. *Pretty please, Gloria… do not talk about…*

"Well, the first time I met Emmy,"—Gloria's tremulous voice cut off Emmy's silent prayer—"it was a disaster. Her treats were just awful. She was auditioning for a spot at the Glensheen's Annual Masquerade Ball. She brought us these wilted-looking lumps that were supposed to be pumpkins. But that wasn't the bad part. When we bit into them, the dye from the sweet turned our teeth orange! I couldn't remove the stain for the better part of a week. It was terrible."

While Gloria rambled on about the party pumpkin debacle, Pierce looked on in sympathy. As the scene rolled out, Emmy sat with her head in her hands trying to steady her breathing. And then, just like that it was done. A commercial was playing and everyone in the room was looking right at her.

"Did that actually happen?" Callie Ann asked, her hand pressed to her Southern heart as if she might faint.

Emmy nodded.

"You poor dear," Silvia said. Emmy's eyes filled with tears.

"And you still stayed in business?" Marguerite asked coldly.

Again, Emmy nodded. "It was rough for a bit. I learned a lot in those first few months. I was able to redeem myself in time for the New Year's Gala, where they featured my signature hot cocoa bar. I wish they would have shown some footage of Gloria talking about that instead. Or our paint and sip classes with the kids, or... or..."

"Or anything but that," said Marguerite, her distaste clearly conveyed in her tone.

"Yeah," Emmy said, feeling defeated. "Anything but that."

~

Emmy watched the rest of the episode in zombie mode. The corners of her vision were shadowed, and her hands gripped the edge of the couch to keep her from falling down a black hole of despair. She didn't blame Gloria. She had probably been baited. She probably had said a hundred other lovely things about Emmy. The fact that Dixie didn't choose any of that footage was not poor sweet Gloria's fault. Emmy knew this. For the remainder of the airing Emmy reminded herself of this fact again and again, hoping it would sink in so that she wouldn't have to add hate to the growing list of negative emotions she was currently experiencing.

When Gerard's section ended, "on-screen Pierce" stood up from his fancy chair, walked toward the front hall, and ushered the TV viewing audience out of the mansion. Before they "left," he invited them back tomorrow night, and each night this week, to watch the competition unfold and build to the finale that would take place on Saturday night,

Valentine's Day.

"No need to make any fancy reservations," he cooed. "We'll be expecting you right here, where life is as sweet as you make it."

The cameras zoomed over his head and out the front door where it was now dark, except for the fountain that was now lit and glowing beautifully. The camera dashed toward it, and seemingly through it, only to spin one hundred and eighty degrees to look back at the enchantingly lit mansion as it grew smaller and smaller, until the screen faded to black.

The delicate sound of ascending chimes, a sound that reminded Emmy of Tinkerbell, cut the silence of the room. The sound signaled the show's credits, with Dixie's name first, surrounded by the spritzing glitter that accompanied the magical cookbook in the intro shots. On cue, Dixie walked to the front of the room and muted the volume on the TV. The credits rolled across the screen with increasing speed.

"Lovely, just lovely!" she cheered and applauded. The others, not sure what else to do, looked around the room and joined in the clapping. "It was exactly as I had envisioned. Now, a few rules."

A junior staffer handed around a red dossier, similar to the contestant profile Emmy had read on the plane, but red and much thicker.

"We'll just cover the highlights," Dixie said. "To make sure things run smoothly. You've already signed your contracts, so there's nothing really that can be changed, but just to make sure we are all on the same page, I want to reiterate a few things."

Emmy robotically opened the cover of her folder but couldn't make the words on the page come into focus.

"Every evening a schedule of events for the following day will be delivered to your room. It is your responsibility to show up punctually, dressed for the challenge that lays ahead. Filming crews will be present in an assortment of locations around the estate, which you are not permitted to leave for the duration of your involvement in the competition. There will be no cell phone usage from this moment forward, to either call, text, or post on social media. The emergency contact person on your application forms has been notified of this and has been given my direct number should an emergency at home arise. Our videographers and photographers will be posting their work on the EatTV website, Facebook page, Instagram, Pinterest, and Twitter profiles. Your business managers and assistants can feel free to pull images from those locations to use for your own advertising as they see fit, as long as the EatTV logo remains fully in view. I think that about covers our agenda for this evening. I will see you bright and early tomorrow morning. For now, you are all dismissed."

When Dixie turned to leave the room, Emmy suddenly sprang back to life.

"Dixie, can I talk to you a moment, please?" The words were out of her mouth before she had fully formed them in her mind.

Dixie stopped and turned around slowly. She held the folder of rules tightly against her chest and surveyed Emmy with an icy glare.

"What was that?" Emmy asked, pointing to

the now dark TV screen.

"I beg your pardon?" Dixie asked.

"Everyone else got beautiful interviews. Glowing fans and rave reviews! You emailed me two hours before Pierce showed up and goaded an old lady into telling horror stories about me! It was awful!"

Dixie pursed her lips and looked as if she were pondering how to respond. She reached out and tried to take Emmy by the hand, but Emmy recoiled.

"Darling," Dixie said. "Did you ever watch *American Idol*?"

"What does that have to do with anything?" Emmy asked.

"Just answer the question."

"Yes."

"You know at the very beginning of the show when they show these hopeful, starstruck singers… who think they're finally going to make it big in the world? And then they're just plain awful?" Here she paused for dramatic effect. "That's you. Everyone else here is well established. They are pros. They are brilliant in the kitchen. You, my dear, are the comedic relief."

Emmy could hear the jaws behind her drop. Whether due to the realization of this truth or the fact that it was stated so bluntly, Emmy would never know.

"My missing driver? My late departure time? The last-minute email? My missing luggage?"

"The luggage was not my doing," Dixie said devilishly. "Just the universe playing along."

Emmy stood still for a second, needing to

gather her thoughts before she spoke next.

"I need to know right now that in the kitchen, in the competition, despite all that you have done to stack the deck against me, I get a fair shot. If I can prove that I belong here, I want to know that I will get to stay. I want your word that the meddling ends, right now."

"Darling, I have no idea what you are talking about," said Dixie, feigning innocence. It's just been a string of bad luck for you. And we all feel just terrible for it. Maybe a good night's sleep will do you well. Tomorrow's a new day, and life is as sweet as you make it." Dixie leaned around Emmy to look at the rest of the flabbergasted contestants. "Good night, y'all. See ya in the mornin'."

~

It was not the first time Emmy wished there was an instruction manual to help her navigate life. Whereas *Candy Making For Dummies* had helped launch her chocolatier career, and *Instructions for a Broken Heart* had metaphorically saved her life in college—twice—there was likely no book on a Barnes and Noble shelf entitled: *How Normal People Successfully Make It on a National Reality TV Series*. She wanted desperately to succeed on the show, and now as she lay in bed on the night after her first episode, she wished for a $27.99 consumable self-help pep talk.

Since she was not likely to find any such manual, especially this time of night, she lay in bed, drafting a copy of the instructional manual she wished she had, hoping that these mental notes would be enough to help her survive the following day.

How Not to Embarrass Myself on National Television, While Playing a Role I Am Vastly Underqualified to Play. An Instruction Manual to Myself, By Emmy Dawson

Rule #1: Be camera ready at a moment's notice. Always brush AND floss your teeth post meal. Apply copious amounts of antiperspirant. Bed head and dry shampoo are no longer acceptable. Panty lines and bra straps are tacky. Keep your undergarments under control at all times.

Rule #2: Do not be a drama queen. Do not, under any circumstances, throw kitchen utensils. Remember during post-show interviews to never, ever, ever cry. Tears are never a good look for anyone.

Rule #3: Show up on time, ready to go. Be professional and they will treat you likewise. At least, the snarky producer and two-faced host will have less grounds to hate you, and therefore kick you off the show before you actually deserve to go. The best strategy for winning is doing the work well.

Rule #4: No foul language in the kitchen. The exclamatory phrase "Holy Shitballs!" should never leave your mouth on national television, especially when chocolate is in the vicinity.

Rule #5: Channel your inner duck. Even if your little

legs are churning furiously beneath the water, appear calm and collected on the surface. Nobody needs to know when you are freaking out. Nobody.

Rule #6: Under no circumstances whatsoever are you allowed to think of past failures. Do not mention them. They do not exist. Even though the whole world now knows you once dyed an entire advisory board's teeth orange via the excessive use of food coloring, do not speak of it. That highly embarrassing and reputation-damaging incident is in the past, and that's where it should stay.

Rule #7: Be nice to the people who could make you look bad. AKA the aforementioned snarky producer and two-faced host. But, be even nicer to the people who could make you look good. Plain and simple: make friends with the make-up crew tomorrow morning, ASAP.

Rule #8: Remember Midwest manners have just as much pull as Southern charm. Stay true to yourself. A damn good cup of hot cocoa is just as good as a piece of key lime pie.

Emmy recited the list to herself again and again, until eventually each rule was ingrained in her brain, and frequently punctuated by a yawn. Look good. No drama. Stay calm. Be professional. Stay positive. Be nice. Repeat. Right now her goal wasn't even to win the competition, it was simply to stay in the competition.

It couldn't be that hard, could it?

February 9

Chapter 10

Emmy awoke in the morning to her alarm. If she held very still and didn't think too hard, she could stay wrapped inside the lovely little bubble of warmth and hazy morning light. But the second her mind flipped to the day ahead, yesterday's events came crashing down on her.

She played her portion of the episode over again in her head, immediately followed by the scene of Dixie telling her that she would certainly be the first to go. Dixie's final line stuck in her head, probably because she and Eddie and Rachel had been sarcastically using the phrase anytime something was less than perfect.

When Rachel accidentally tipped over a bowl of caramel sauce on the counter? "Life is as sweet as you make it, Rach!" Emmy sweetly sang as she walked out to help a customer at the front counter.

When Emmy dropped her car keys into the freezing slush that pooled by her tires in the parking lot, Eddie had coyly goaded her as she took off her mittens and dipped them into the puddle to retrieve them. "Bummer, sweetie. I don't want to hear complaints of cold fingers though. Life is as sweet as you make it."

When Eddie realized they were out of ranch and he'd therefore have to eat his buffalo wings sans dressing, Emmy rubbed his back and said, "So sorry, sweetheart. But you'll survive. Life is as sweet as you make it."

Life is as sweet at you make it. Life is as sweet as you make it. As annoying as it might be, it was pretty darn true. And right now, it was the best advice Emmy could give herself. Life is as sweet as you make it. She threw off her covers and was determined to face the day without a trace of bitterness.

And then she remembered she didn't have her suitcase. Her backpack contained her toiletries, so at least she would be physically clean on the most basic levels, but Emmy wasn't sure if that was enough. She grabbed the day's agenda, which had been shoved under the door after she went to sleep, and then climbed back into bed.

Sitting up, surrounded by copious amounts of pillows, Emmy read over the events of the day ahead.

Breakfast 9:00 a.m.
Contestant Meeting 9:45 a.m.
Hair and Make-Up Consultations 10:30 a.m.
Lunch 12:30 p.m.
Report for Hair and Make-Up 3:00 p.m.
Pre-Show Shots 4:30 p.m.
Live filming begins 6:00 p.m.
Voting opens 7:00 p.m.
Filming ends: 8:00 p.m.
Post-Show Meeting 8:05 p.m.
Late Dinner 8:15 p.m.

Emmy looked at her watch. She had one hour until breakfast. This place had to have a gift shop, right? She could acquire clean clothes there and then rush back to shower. It sounded like as good a plan as any. Emmy didn't waste time. She threw on yesterday's clothes, shoved her feet in her shoes, and was out the door with her credit card in hand.

It turned out that "gift shop" wasn't exactly the right term. The Biltmore had more of a gift *village*. As Emmy dashed across the cobblestones from one picturesque window front to the next, she discovered the same thing over and over again. Locked doors. Dark interiors. The stores did not open until nine o'clock.

She slumped down onto a bench and leaned her head back against the still cool brick.

"Well, it *had* been a good plan," she mumbled.

"What was a good plan?"

A woman's voice jolted Emmy out of her slump. She stood up and found a petite woman, the quintessential fairy godmother of a woman, standing before the side entrance of the store Emmy had finally given up at.

"My luggage was lost, yesterday at the airport. I'm supposed to be on this show today, but all I have to wear are the clothes I traveled in yesterday." Emmy pulled at her baggy sweater, that could now more accurately be described as drooping and saggy. "I was hoping to find some new clothes here, so that I didn't look quite so…" Emmy's voice trailed off, unable to find the adjective that truly described how she felt on the inside and out. In the end she just held up her arms and shrugged.

"Well, we can't have that. The estate is

thrilled to be hosting the EatTV contest and we can't have any ragamuffins on the screen, now can we?" The woman winked at Emmy. "Come on in here, hunnie; use the side door. We'll get you fixed up in no time."

The woman, who introduced herself as Judy, ushered Emmy into the store and straight to the dressing room.

"I'll just bring you some things."

Even though she had just met Judy, Emmy had zero fear that the clothes the store attendant brought her would be unstylish. She had never before seen a woman in her sixties so impeccably dressed. Confident she was in safe hands, Emmy complied.

"Size 6!" Emmy yelled over the top of the dressing room door as she started to peel off her layers.

In a matter of minutes Emmy had two complete outfits, one casual and one professional.

Just as Judy rang up the total and Emmy was about to swipe her credit card, Judy threw up her hands.

"Wait!" she cried.

Judy dashed to the back of the store faster than Emmy thought possible. When she returned, Judy held a gorgeous apron in her hands. She slid it from the hanger and placed the strap around Emmy's neck. The muslin fabric made it seem lighter than air. A single delicate ruffle graced the collar and was mimicked in the curved scallops on the bottom. Across the chest in looping cursive were the words "from the Kitchen of the Vanderbilts."

"It's perfect!" Judy cooed. "My gift! To you! A

good-luck charm!"

Again, Emmy tried to protest.

"Nonsense. Besides, now I have someone to cheer for. Hasn't anyone told you it's more fun if you have some skin in the game? Just wait until the other girls arrive at the store to work. They'll be green with envy that I got to meet you. Tonight, we are all watching the show at Meredith's house. We'll all make sure to vote for you!"

Emmy thanked her profusely and continued to do so until Judy shooed her out of the shop.

"Go on now! You have a competition to win!"

Emmy ran back toward the mansion while waving over her shoulder, thanking the lord that good people still existed in this world.

~

At 8:59, when Emmy slid into her spot at the breakfast table, showered and in clean clothes, Dixie Champlain raised her eyebrows. Emmy gave her a Cheshire grin, picked up her fork, and began to eat the breakfast before her. As she polished off the whole-wheat pancake topped with gorgonzola cheese and baked cinnamon apples, she leaned back completely content. It was hard to relate to the earlier panic-crazed version of herself.

Food fixes so many things, Emmy thought to herself. She was able to maintain her good mood throughout Dixie's morning speech, which was mostly a repeat from her presentation last night. A reminder of basic rules, a rundown of today's schedule, and a healthy dose of EatTV propaganda about sweet lives and big prizes. When she was finished, everyone politely clapped. Emmy looked around the table and saw the competitive streaks sparkle to life in each person's eyes. This was it.

Within seconds of Dixie's conclusion, dishes were whisked away, and contestants were directed to the different rooms about the mansion to meet with their individual hair and make-up team. On her way out to a guest bedroom, Emmy saw Callie Ann literally jump up and down and squeal as a woman who could have been her twin clasped her hands tightly and smothered her with compliments.

Emmy tried to ignore her feelings of annoyance and told herself that Callie Ann could look as pretty as she wanted; she still had to make good candy in order to win this competition. Emmy wished that she believed herself. She was just about to spiral into another tunnel of doubt when she walked into her assigned room.

Her jaw dropped. The room was amazing. Incredible. Stupendous. Emmy ran her hand along the intricately patterned wallpaper and trailed her fingers on the velvet fabric of the divan. She ogled the gold-leafed mirror and picked up an ivory hairbrush laid out on a silver tray. All thoughts of Callie Ann and her beauty went out the door, down the hall, and disappeared somewhere in the ancient home. Amidst the opulence, there was no room to be in awe of more than a single item at a time, and at this moment, Callie Ann was not it.

"You must be Emmy," said a woman stepping forward with her hand extended. Emmy snapped out of her trance and met her halfway across the room. "I'm Magnolia."

"Magnolia?" Emmy repeated, wanting to be sure

she heard the woman correctly.

"Darling, in this industry, your name means everything." Magnolia put up her hand and stage whispered to Emmy as she pulled her across the room, "If my resume listed Maggie Sue, you can bet your bottom dollar I would not be here in this room with you right now." She winked mischievously.

"Magnolia it is," Emmy said with a smile. Emmy made a mental note to tell Maggie the story about her own naming as each woman took a seat on the edge of a lush sofa.

"Alrighty, let's get down to work. It's my job to make you look magnificent on-screen. I'm thinking your hair pulled back, maybe with a braid or twist? We want to keep the look consistent through each episode, so America can easily recognize you and then obviously fall in love with you."

Emmy nodded along as Magnolia made plans aloud. When a Biltmore staff member walked in and delivered Emmy's "lost" luggage, Emmy knew things were definitely starting to look up.

Chapter 11

The hours between breakfast and the filming melted away. Before she knew it, Emmy was standing in the kitchen surrounded by the other contestants and more cameras than she could count. With her legs shaking and her hands sweating, she tried to remind herself to breathe. Had she ever been this nervous? Seconds into a personal montage of all the other nerve-wracking moments in her life, Emmy told herself to knock it off.

She had already been interviewed in her kitchen space during the pre-show shots. She told Pierce about her newbie jitters, her hopes for the competition, and her plans for the prize money and cookbook. It was a nice way to start. Pierce even allowed her to start over once when she got tongue-tied. This film would be mined for clips and inserted throughout the evening's episode. Maybe he wasn't such a bad guy after all.

But the real show was about to start.

"Welcome back to the beautiful Biltmore Estate," Pierce said with a broad smile. He stood, beaming, in front of the eight contestants. "Tonight, we will learn more about our contestants and test their candy-making skills to find out…" Here he paused dramatically while the music reached a crescendo and then cut off entirely. "The Vanderbilt Valentine's Day Candy-Making Champion!"

The camera swept along the line of competitors, taking in their excited, nervous, and expectant expressions.

"For our first challenge, you will be asked to

make a candy classic." Again, a dramatic pause. "A lollipop." Again, the camera sweep of the competitor's faces. Marguerite distinctly wrinkled her nose while Callie Ann could be described as positively giddy. Otis wrung his hands like an evil genius while Jean Luc nodded thoughtfully. Andy, Silvia, and Gerard smiled like they knew exactly how they were going to win this challenge. Emmy's face was stoic, already mentally planning her moves. She did not have time to waste.

Emmy could feel her eyes drifting to the ingredients that lined the shelves at the far end of the kitchen, but she pulled them back. Emmy forced herself to listen to Pierce's full set of challenge instructions.

"You will be given one hour to make your lollipops and present them to your judge for the evening—me! Then, based on my assessment of the sweets and their visible presentation, all of America will phone in to vote. I wish you the best on this first challenge and remember, life is as sweet as you make it!"

As Pierce finished speaking, a loud horn sounded, scaring the contestants badly. Silvia actually yelped aloud, and Marguerite brought her hands to her chest in shock. But the rest of the contestants were off and running to the ingredients. Andy was out front, giggling like a sugar-high madman. A few feet before the shelves he launched himself on the floor and slid face-first toward the fully stocked shelves. Seconds before crashing, he pulled himself upright and started snatching ingredients. Emmy arrived next and locked eyes with Andy. They both smiled and then rushed to their stations to begin.

Emmy grabbed two bars of milk chocolate, two bars of dark chocolate, a baggie of confetti heart sprinkles and a tiny bottle of toasted coconut flavoring. After depositing her ingredients on her work space, Emmy grabbed two small saucepans and placed them on the stove on low heat. She broke the chocolate bars into pieces and tossed them into the pot, milk chocolate in one, dark chocolate in the other. While they slowly melted, Emmy pulled out a cookie sheet and covered it in parchment paper.

"Sticks!" Emmy suddenly shouted and scrambled back to the supply shelves for this absolutely crucial element. Apparently, she wasn't the only one who had forgotten this crucial element. Upon hearing her exclamation, Jean Luc and Callie Ann rushed back as well, with Gerard closely behind.

"Oops, so sorry, Gerard," Callie Ann sang out. "None left!" She waved the final sucker sticks in his famous face.

"Callie Ann, may I please?" Gerard asked. "Just two. Do you really need all twelve in that package?"

"I'm making a lolli-bouquet," she said with an air of superiority. "Yes."

"Really?" Gerard asked again.

"Really," Callie Ann said and strode off in the direction of her work space.

Gerard shook his head and then moved on in search of a few spare sticks. Marguerite, the closest to the supplies, also denied him. So did Otis. Jean Luc had only taken four, and Silvia had already placed her sticks into her candy molds and could not remove them without damaging her final product. By the time Gerard stood huffing and puffing in front of Emmy, he was desperate.

"Emmy," he begged, "please, can I have some of your sticks?"

"No problem, Gerard." Emmy held out six sticks. "I'm only using half of my package. Is six enough?"

"You're a saint!" Gerard said, snatching the sticks from her outstretched hand. "Thank you!"

Emmy turned from Gerard's disappearing figure and added two drops of flavoring to the dark chocolate pot and stirred both varieties with her spatula. She then poured the contents of each into a broadcloth piping bag. In alternating turns Emmy swirled strings of the melted chocolate onto the parchment paper. Milk chocolate, dark. Milk chocolate, dark. After several rounds she placed a sucker stick in the center of each doily of chocolate and then repeated the process, adding several more layers. Finally, Emmy dusted each lollipop with a pinch of the festively colored sprinkles she had selected and placed them on a rack to cool in the refrigerator.

Emmy glanced up at the large clock looming above the set. It was strange to see so many modern items mixed in with the antiquities of the old kitchen. The cameras and their lenses, the fancy mixers and state-of-the-art ovens. They looked ridiculous in contrast to the century-old tile and the rack of overhanging pots. Despite the absurdity of the era-conflicting appliances, Emmy was incredibly thankful to be cooking with modern utensils. There's no way she'd be able to battle her nerves and all-star competitors cooking like the original Vanderbilts. Or at least like the original Vanderbilts' staff!

Five minutes remained. Emmy watched the clock click from 4:59 to 5:00 and then pulled her suckers from the refrigerator. She looked around her space for a unique way to display her treats. An empty milk bottle caught her eye, and with two minutes left she lifted the suckers from the parchment paper and placed them carefully into the bottle.

It looks pretty good, she thought, pleased with herself. *But it could use one final touch...*

Emmy ran to the shelves one last time and pulled the red ribbon from a sack of wheat flour. She dashed back to her station and tied it around the neck of the bottle just as the timer expired.

Again, the obnoxious horn sounded.

"Candy makers!" Pierce called throughout the kitchen. "Time's up!"

~

When Emmy looked at the lineup of treats, she didn't quite know how to feel. Or maybe, she didn't know which emotion to give full attention, because so many of them struggled for attention at the same time.

Emmy was proud. Her lollipops looked cute. Sweet. Like a Valentine's Day treat.

Emmy was in awe. Silvia's red wine lollies were dusted with actual flecks of gold and positively sparkled in the set lights.

Emmy was nervous. How would her sucker stand up to the others?

Emmy was relieved. Gerard's treats looked like lumps of dirt. He'd tried to cover them with shredded coconut, but even to Emmy's rookie eyes, they were a mess.

Pierce came up with the same assessment. He declared Silvia's suckers divine and Callie Ann's bouquet of colorful gumdrop blooms ingenious. He was skeptical of Otis's suckers made of alternating layers of seaweed and lime-flavored fruit strips. But as Pierce put the interesting green concoction into his mouth, his face morphed from apprehension to surprised joy. Jean Luc and Marguerite also got favorable reactions for their creations. Andy's suckers featuring miniature puffs of cotton candy in pinks and purple were deemed delightful. Pierce didn't even want to eat Gerard's treat, but was obligated by contract.

"What happened?" Pierce asked Gerard. Their faces might as well have adorned the cover of a funeral planning brochure. They were already in the process of mourning the culinary tragedy that sat before them.

"The chocolate burned," Gerard said, eyeing a few of the contestants malevolently. "Overcooked, while I was trying to find sticks."

"That's too bad," Pierce said. And for a moment Emmy almost believed he was being sincere.

For Emmy's sucker he said, "While the on the outside your treat looks like something special, it tastes simple. You could have done more."

The competitors were told to stand behind

their treat as Pierce asked the viewers to call in and vote. It was an awkward and nerve-wracking fifteen minutes. During the one commercial break Emmy turned to Silvia.

"Your suckers look amazing!" Emmy complimented.

"Thank you!" Silvia beamed. "They are some of my favorites. A great treat for ladies' get-togethers. Book clubs love them. You don't actually catch a buzz off the red wine I use to make them, but I don't exactly advertise that!"

"Shhhh!" Dixie scolded the pair. "Coming back in three, two…" Dixie mouthed the word one and pointed to Pierce to take over.

"Well, ladies and gentlemen, the hour is upon us. The voting lines closed just a few moments ago, and our trusted staff of numerical analysts have provided me with the name of the candy maker going home. But first, congratulations are in order!"

The music swelled, and Pierce leaned forward on his toes, increasing the tension of the moment. Pierce pinched his lips, holding back the announcement.

"Congratulations to… Silvia, the winner of our first challenge. Your decadent red wine lollipops were delicious, and a treat the Vanderbilts would have truly loved."

The other contestants clapped politely, and Silvia smiled and nodded her head magnanimously.

"Unfortunately," said Pierce, sobering the moment instantly, "not everyone has been so successful tonight. Emmy and Gerard, please step forward. Your two treats earned the lowest number of votes this evening and so, one of you must go home."

Emmy stepped forward on shaky legs. Dixie had warned her this would happen. Emmy did not listen to Pierce reassess her challenge creation or Gerard's. Instead she willed herself not to cry. She told herself to keep her chin up, to smile. She told herself that she did her best. Truly she did. And if that was not good enough to stay, then so be it.

"The candy maker going home tonight is…" Pierce hung his head and waited for the music. That damn music. Emmy held her breath. Down at her sides she crossed her fingers and didn't care that it made her feel as if she were back in the sixth grade hoping not to be chosen last for teams in recess. The music cut, and a silence filled the kitchen space. It probably lasted for a second, but to Emmy it felt like an eternity. Finally, Pierce picked up his head, looked right at Emmy and said, "Gerard Taylor."

~

Twenty minutes later, the cameras had all gone and only the contestants, Pierce, and Dixie remained in the studio kitchen. Emmy returned to her station to clean her space. It was there, as she stacked her dirty dishes in the collection bin for some lowly intern to wash, that Dixie stopped by.

"Pretty lucky today," Dixie said and jerked her head toward Gerard, who was angrily stuffing his apron into his messenger bag. Emmy took a deep breath and turned to face the producer.

"I think I did well," Emmy said. "I'm proud of what I created."

"Really?" Dixie asked with mock sincerity.

"Yes. Really," Emmy spat.

Dixie shook her head as if Emmy were the one out of touch. "Well, don't expect it to last, sweetheart."

Dixie patted her on the shoulder and then hip checked her into the counter, causing her chocolate-covered pans and utensils to clatter to the floor. Chocolate and sprinkles splattered across every inch of her allotted space.

Emmy stood there dumbfounded. Maybe she really was back in middle school.

Back in her room Emmy wanted to do anything but think. Thinking only made her crabby and annoyed. This entire competition had been rigged, and the more she thought about the details of the day and her time here at the Biltmore, the more she read into every teeny, tiny little action. Every passing glance, every single comment, every incident of bad luck. Had it been luck? Or had it been planned?

Turning the events over and over in her mind was getting her nowhere. She needed a distraction. For the third time since leaving the studio kitchen, she reached for her phone, wanting to call Eddie or her mom, wanting to text Rachel or her best friend, Anna, back in the cities. And then she remembered that her phone was in her suitcase, turned off, so that it wouldn't tempt her to break the rules and "communicate with the outside world." As she paced her room inside the mansion, she felt trapped. Sure, this was a beautiful prison cell, but it really wasn't much more than that.

Emmy, knock it off. Are you kidding me? A

prison cell? She scolded herself. *How many times at home would you have killed for a night 100 percent*
off and to yourself? Haven't you asked for this exact situation like a thousand times in the past year?

Enjoy it!

Emmy decided to go for a walk. Her meandering from hall to hall and room to room had brought her to the library. If Emmy had been impressed by The Biltmore before, it was nothing compared to the admiration she felt now. Solid walls of bookshelves stretched for three solid floors, a spiral staircase giving access to each floor in turn. In Emmy's mind she saw Belle, from *Beauty and the Beast*, slide across the room on a caster in song. This place, this collection, this sheer volume of gathered ink and paper and knowledge was... magnificent.

She walked among the rows and rows of books. She let her fingers trail over the antique spines. She admired their leather covers and gold-leafed title inscriptions. She even bent over and smelled one or two books. As much as she wanted to feel sophisticated by reading one of George Vanderbilt's books, none of them called to her the way the book in her backpack did. Deciding that her anger was spent, or more likely snuffed out by pure wonderment, Emmy made her way back to her room. Once there, she crossed the plush carpet to her carry-on and pulled out a ragged copy of *A Wrinkle in Time* from the front zipper.

She slipped between the covers and sunk into the abundance of pillows.

It was a dark and stormy night.

There was something about reading about Meg's adolescent drama, her insecurities, her family turmoil, her battle with an epic-sized evil force, that made Emmy's own troubles seem tiny. If Meg could find a way to overcome her seemingly insurmountable obstacles, then Emmy could too.

Emmy read late into the night. Finally, after Meg met the Happy Medium and let her anger overpower her fear, Emmy closed the book, turned off her bedside light, and fell asleep. She dreamed of a giant evil Dixie. Clad in billowing black robes, she towered over the mansion and barked orders across the expanse of the eight thousand acres. Just before she awoke, Emmy defeated the diabolical Dixie by serving her the sweetest treat, with the biggest smile.

February 10

Chapter 12

When she awoke Emmy stretched and smiled. She knew how she would get through this. The same way she had gotten through sixth grade. She was going to kill 'em all with kindness. While Magnolia twisted Emmy's auburn hair into a braid, she told the stylist about her interactions with the producer and her suspicions of treachery right from the start.

"Whoa, whoa, whoa," Magnolia said and locked eyes with Emmy in the mirror. "I know nothing about this. I swear."

"I didn't mean to accuse you." Emmy spun around in the chair and looked at Magnolia with a sinking feeling in her gut.

What if my stylist really is in on the scandal too? she thought in horror.

Emmy stared into her eyes. Magnolia crossed her heart and put up three fingers in a Girl Scout salute.

"Are you even a real Girl Scout?" Emmy asked.

"Gold Award recipient." Magnolia stared back.

"Me too!" Emmy said and held up her hand for a high five. Magnolia slapped her hand and then turned her around and continued braiding. The awkwardness of the moment evaporated when Magnolia suggested Emmy start leaving Dixie special notes around the set, letting her know that her leadership skills were positively inspiring.

"Oh, Magnolia, you are good!" Emmy praised.

"Please, in here, call me Maggie."

Emmy nodded. "Or maybe I could make an extra treat each challenge, just for her? I now know saltwater taffy is her favorite, even if she claims not to eat candy anymore."

"No, no, no," Maggie cut in. "How about you give her a shout-out on camera, saying how special she has made this experience for you."

The two were near tears when Maggie finally made them stop and be serious, so she could apply Emmy's eyeliner. After an hour together, Emmy left her room feeling, and looking, better than ever.

~

"Tonight's competition will be judged by couples visiting the estate to celebrate Valentine's Day. You will have three hours to create a dozen batches of sweets to serve via kiosks in the Antler Hill Village. There will be two opportunities to win today's challenge. Whichever contestant runs out of their treat first and whoever gets the best reviews will win the challenge. Your time... starts... now!"

Pierce stepped to the side and swept his arm horizontally, allowing the competitors to rush past him to the freshly stocked shelves of ingredients. As the six other contestants scrambled to fill their arms with ingredients faster than Go Go Gadget arms, Emmy stood and calculated. Her eyes bounced from shelf to shelf, taking in the contents. When the last competitor stepped away and Emmy had full view of the shelves, she began to cherry-pick the leftovers.

"Looks like someone's getting a slow start," Pierce said over her shoulder.

"I'm working smarter, not harder, Pierce," Emmy said confidently. She flashed him a smile over her shoulder. He'd only been in Emmy's dream for a moment, a tentacle extension of the evil that was destroyed by the same sweetness as Dixie. "Trust the process."

Back at her station Emmy unloaded kabob sticks, gelatin, and heart-shaped molds. She took out a cake pan, dumped the sticks in a shallow pool of water, and added a few drops of cinnamon graham flavoring from the treat mixology kit stocked at her kitchen. While the sticks soaked, she filled a pot of water and set it to boil. Once it did, she added the gelatin and filled the heart-shaped molds.

As the gelatin set, Emmy removed the sticks and rolled them in pink, finely crushed sugar and set them to the side. Next, she made the marshmallows. She lined her pans with tin foil and coated them with vegetable oil spray. Then, in her mixer she combined water with another package of gelatin. As those ingredients sat patiently, Emmy boiled water, corn syrup, sugar, and salt and then poured them into the mixer as well. The ingredients folded in on themselves over and over again, becoming thicker and stickier by the minute. When the mixture was almost complete, Emmy added two teaspoons of vanilla extract and then poured it into her awaiting pans.

"Any tips for our viewers at home?" Pierce asked over her shoulder.

"Speed is your friend," Emmy said as she used a spatula to swipe the sides of her metal mixing bowl. "If the marshmallow cools off too much, it makes a huge mess."

"I see," Pierce said as a camera zoomed for a closer look at Emmy's dispersing technique. "What is the next step?"

"I'll sift cornstarch and confectioner's sugar over the top to give it an additional blast of sweetness, and then I'm going to… well, can't a girl have any secrets?"

"Never," Pierce said, grinning devilishly.

"Oh, alright," Emmy said good-naturedly. "I'm going to cut them out using these heart-shaped cookie cutters, and then I'll finally be ready to assemble my kabobs."

"We'll leave you to it," Pierce said, his eyes already on the next station, the next contestant, the next invasive interview. "Good luck, Emmy!"

With the marshmallows lined up along her workstation, she punched out one fluffy heart after another. She removed the gelatin from the molds and then filled them again. She repeated the process again and again.

Finally, she assembled her candy kabobs one sweet piece at a time. As she put her dessert together, she looked around the kitchen. Her eyes went first to Jean Luc. He was humming and actually kicking up his heels as he cooked in his kitchen space. Emmy couldn't see exactly what he was making, but it looked like it was making Jean Luc very, very happy.

Marguerite was taste testing a bit of custard filling from a ramekin with a tiny spoon. Displeased by what encountered her taste buds, she shook more cinnamon into the steaming pot. Silvia's station was covered in chocolate drops, and Otis had all four burners and the oven going in his station. Callie Ann's station was an explosion of color, and Andy was busy lining up snow-cone cups.

As each contestant passed her station, on their way to the supplies or refrigerator or bathroom, Emmy asked them how their treat was coming along and wished them luck. The clock clicked down, and Emmy continued to assemble. When the last gummy was finally skewered, Emmy tied the shish kabobs together in pairs with strands of shoestring licorice, finishing off each perfect pair of treats with a beautiful red bow.

~

Two hours later, the crowds of couples had cleared out from the village, and the contestants stood huddled together, waiting for instructions from Dixie and Pierce. For a minute, they all felt like winners. The guests had so many nice things to say about their candies, and everyone was feeling confident enough to be gracious and civil.

"I was so busy at my little station, I didn't even get to see what everyone else made!" Callie Ann said. For once, Emmy thought she sounded sincere.

"You know that old movie, *Chitty Chitty Bang Bang*?" Emmy asked her. "The movie about the flying car? Well, there's a scene when the crazy inventor guy makes these whistling treats."

"Oh, yes! I remember," Otis said cheerfully.

"But it all backfires and brings the dogs to the candy factory!"

"Well, Jean Luc actually pulled it off," Andy said with admiration. "He made a candy that actually whistles. He's a genius!"

"It was also super annoying and unfortunately copyrighted," Dixie clipped, joining the conversation. "It's a nightmare. We can't show any of his footage at the risk of being sued."

She didn't wait to see the other contestants' reactions. Dixie turned to face Jean Luc and began berating him. Jean Luc's face fell. His hands came up as he tried to explain, to defend, to convince. But it was no use. Dixie would not hear it. Any of it.

"This is unforgiveable. How could you possibly think this was a good idea?" She shook her finger at him. "I don't care what the votes say. You are off the show." Then she stormed off as fast as her stilettos would allow.

When Dixie left, Emmy rushed to Jean Luc, who was now standing with his head in his hands.

"Oh, Jean Luc," Emmy consoled. "Don't listen to her. I think your treats were wonderful."

~

"Before we get to the moment of truth," Pierce said with all of his usual gusto, "let me give you an insider's look at the competition today." Emmy wasn't sure how they were able to pipe the music into the open-air marketplace, but there it was, as dramatic as ever.

The screens of viewers all across the nation cut to footage from the Biltmore kitchens. They saw the mad dash for the ingredients and the contestants working at their individual stations. They saw Pierce popping into talk with several of the contestants, although not Jean Luc. Emmy was happy with her answers to Pierce's questions, but somehow her time on-screen was still manipulated to portray her as the underdog.

Pierce skipped his in-depth assessment of each treat and instead Dixie filled the time with mini interviews Pierce had done with the visiting couples. Gorgeous and in love, they made for excellent viewing pleasure. As the contestants stood behind their treats and listened to the played-back interviews, it was hard to feel nervous. They already knew the results—at least, the important one. Poor Jean Luc already had tears streaming down his face. Footage of everyone's sweet made it onto the screen, except Jean Luc's. For a brief moment, patrons were seen in line at his mini-store, but as they brought the whistling sweet to their lips, the camera cut back to Jean Luc's expectant face.

"Look alive, ya'll, we're coming back in five, four, three…" From behind a camera crew member, Dixie finished the countdown with her well-manicured fingers. When she got to one, she pointed to Pierce and he took over.

"Earlier I promised you two winners, but I'm sorry, tonight I'll have to disappoint you. You see, the same person won both challenges tonight. Not only did the winning candy maker run out of sweets first, but he—or she—also got the best reviews from our special Vanderbilt guests." The music swelled and then ceased. "Congratulations are in order for the fabulous Callie Ann Collins!"

Callie Ann curtsied and blew a kiss to the camera. Marguerite, on her left, leaned in and gave her a gracious nod, while Otis on her right shook her hand. The rest of the contestants turned in her general direction and offered up their congratulations.

Pierce drew them back to attention with his next words. "Now for the less pleasant news. In my hands I hold the name of the candy maker who received the fewest phone-in votes. The name of the candy maker who must go home."

For a second Emmy wondered if Dixie had been lying.

Is Dixie really sending Jean Luc home… or is she just luring me into a false sense of security so that she can hit me with a Mac truck of devastation? Do they doctor the voting numbers? How can they really calculate the totals so fast?

Her head spun, and with all the questions tumbling around in her brain, she was no longer listening to Pierce.

She felt the shift of Andy next to her as he turned to see Jean Luc walk over to Pierce, shake his hand, and then walk off camera. Suddenly Emmy's eyes filled with tears. Was it because she felt bad for Jean Luc or relieved for herself? Emmy reasoned it had more to do with the powerlessness she felt. All she could do was hang on for the ride. That—and continue to make the best candy she could.

February 11

Chapter 13

At breakfast the following morning, Dixie announced that today's challenge would be a team effort. With a snap of her fingers, a server appeared with a purple velvet bag on a silver tray. Dixie swirled her hand in the air dramatically before plunging it into the depths of the bag to pull out their names, two at a time.

First was Otis and Marguerite.

Then Silvia and Andy.

And finally, Emmy and Callie Ann.

Emmy wasn't sure how to feel. Sure, Callie Ann was a talented candy maker and a competition favorite, but something about her made Emmy nervous. For the hundredth time since arriving, Emmy was reminded of middle school. Of course, you *wanted* to sit at the lunch table of popular girls, but what would they say when you weren't there? Wasn't it better to be out of view, safe from the gossip and fake compliments?

But she didn't have a choice. There was no trading allowed. Before she had time to ponder who she'd rather be partnered with, Dixie began speaking again.

"Today you will each be assigned a storefront in Antler Hill Village. As a team, you will create a delicious looking *and* tasting display. You will have five hours to plan, prepare, and assemble your creation. At 6:30 Biltmore guests will be invited to visit the stores and try your sweets. The voting lines will open at 7:00. Camera crews will be in and out all day, so look alive—we're watching you!" As she said this last line, she pointed to her own eyes and then to the contestants'. Several people laughed openly, but Emmy shuddered. The thought kind of gave her the creeps.

"Please meet your partner in your assigned kitchen station in half an hour. Until then, no talking to your teammate. Between now and then, take care of any personal needs. You are dismissed."

Silvia leaned over to Emmy and said quietly, "I think I'm going to start using that phrase myself. You—crabby customer—I'm done with you. You are dismissed."

Emmy and Silvia giggled, drawing the evil eye of Dixie. Emmy buried her laugh in her cloth napkin. After her sin had been sufficiently stifled, she looked out over the napkin edge at Silvia, who's mischievous eyes mirrored her own.

Right now, as Emmy walked through the front door of the Creamery, an ice cream parlor, that moment felt like a week ago. She looked down at her bedazzled waistline and had second thoughts about her costume. There was really nothing else to call it.

A gigantic poof of tulle wrapped around her waist and shimmering fabric covered every inch of her body. She was a Lycra-clad masterpiece from her hips to her ankles and from her collarbone to her wrists. Speaking of her wrists, several strands of faux jewels encircled them, casting rays of light hither and yon as she walked. The same could be said for the strands that hung from her neck, ears, and—oh God, had she actually agreed to—yes, from her crown.

Magnolia tried her best to put a stop to the foolish display, but Callie Ann and her stylist absolutely refused to budge.

"Well, at least I can make your hair and make-up look good," said Maggie. "And then we'll just have to pray that the crew films you from the neck up as often as possible."

Two steps further in the door Emmy heard a high-pitched squeal.

"Heavens to Betsy! You look adorable!" Callie Ann trilled.

"I'm thirty-one. I don't want to look adorable," Emmy mumbled as she tried and failed to flatten the flounce of her skirt. She looked up at Callie Ann and her jaw dropped. She was gorgeous. In the exact same ridiculous assortment of fabric, Callie Ann looked downright radiant. Royal even! Emmy studied her shrewdly and wondered how she'd done it. Callie Ann took her shocked silence as a compliment.

"I know, right? I was a little nervous at first, but I think I look good. I mean, we do, don't we?" This last phrase she directed at the teenager running the cash register.

One look at his ogling eyes and Emmy knew that the likelihood of coherent speech escaping his lips was slim to none.

"C'mon, c'mon. Let's stand next to the castle for a selfie. I need to get this on Insta, ASAP." Callie Ann tugged on Emmy's wrist. Hard. Emmy did her best to follow quickly, but between her heels and making sure her full skirt didn't catch on any of the tables and chairs, it was a struggle. Emmy looked more like a waddling penguin drenched in glitter than the princess of Callie Ann's vision.

Callie Ann let go of her wrist when they reached the front window display.

Now this is something to admire, Emmy thought. *It's a work of confectionary art!*

Beneath a Styrofoam base, a thinly rolled layer of baby blue gum paste covered the castle from top to bottom. Fastened with piped frosting was a mosaic of candy wafers. Unlike the chalky treats Emmy remembered from her childhood Easter basket, these wafers melted in her mouth.

The first flavor they had created was a malted strawberry. The result was a pastel pink sweet that tasted like a strawberry milkshake. These circles covered the walls and spires of the castle. A periwinkle-colored wafer, with the flavor of lavender-infused lemonade, made up the roof; and just a few white wafers made up the windows and door. The vanilla of these few final wafers was enhanced by the tiniest addition of almond extract. Each wafer was delectable on its own, but when you piled them together and popped them in your mouth, it tasted divine.

All around the castle hung wispy clouds of cotton, suspended on transparent fishing line. While below, tulle lit by fairy lights gave the illusion the castle was floating.

The smile that stretched across Emmy's face morphed into a yawn. Working with Callie Ann had proved to be an emotionally demanding experience, not to mention that for the last hour she had been hunched in awkward angles around the castle, adding the last of the detailed frosting piping. Callie

Ann had left hours before—in search of their outfits, a necessary component that Emmy could not talk her out of. Somehow the camera crew, which had been bustling in and out to check on their progress, had missed most of Emmy's solo efforts. But as Emmy looked at the final product, she decided it was worth it. The long day, the ridiculous outfit, the nagging voice in her head that said this was more of an Emmy product than a team-challenge project... It was worth it because the final result looked perfect. Better than that, it was delicious. To Emmy's ears the castle seemed to sing a song of redemption.

"Say 'winning'!" Callie Ann trilled and held out her arm for a selfie. Emmy leaned in and smiled. Callie Ann snapped the picture and then a few more, with a few different facial expressions, and then buried her face in her screen to select, edit, and post her favorite shot.

The bell on the front door jingled, announcing Dixie's arrival.

"Ladies? Where are you?" she hollered impatiently.

"Up here!" Callie Ann called out while quickly stowing her phone in the folds of her skirt.

Dixie made her way to the front of the store.

"Good lord!" she declared when she laid eyes on them.

Emmy cringed. Dixie was smiling too wide for her judgment to be a good one. The woman showed more love to a disaster than FEMA. And clearly, a disaster is what she thought this was. Two grown women dressed as princesses. She couldn't have loved it more if it were her own idea.

When Dixie walked closer to the window

display, however, her edges softened, and her eyes grew wide.

"Isn't it a dream?" Callie Ann asked. "The dream team, that's what I've been calling us."

Emmy wrinkled her nose. *It would have been nice if you'd told your partner that,* she thought. But by now she knew better than to voice her oppositional opinion in front of these women.

Dixie paced in front of the castle. Silent, scrutinizing, and severe. And then, just when Emmy thought she was about to be scolded and scorned, Dixie spoke.

"I've got to say, ladies," Dixie said quietly. "Well done."

Emmy's heart swelled. After a second of further admiration, Dixie snapped out of her magical daze and spun on her heel to face them.

"We'll just have to see what America thinks of it. The store will open to the Biltmore guests at 6:30. The camera crew arrives shortly after, and voting begins at 7 when we air live. The votes will decide."

~

"Emmy! Emmy! We came to see you!" Judy enveloped Emmy in a hug. Emmy felt a rush of gratitude for her new friend. Seeing a familiar face, even one new to her, buoyed her spirits immensely. "This is my friend Meredith, who works at the store with me."

Once Emmy untangled herself, her jewelry, and a stray bit of tulle sticking to Judy, Meredith and Emmy shook hands.

"Please excuse my outfit, Judy," Emmy said

as she offered them a treat. "My partner insisted. I would have much rather had you dress me."

Further talk of fashion was cut off by the ladies' gushing reviews of the flavored candy wafers.

"Emmy, this is heavenly. I mean it!" Judy declared. "And your display is beautiful. I feel like I am in a fairy tale."

"That's what I"—Emmy paused and, trying to appear like a team player, corrected herself—"I mean, we, were going for."

Emmy pointed toward Callie Ann and the flock of cameras and customers surrounding her. Instead of capturing Callie Ann's natural glow, Emmy wished they would have recorded Judy's praise. Emmy shifted her eyes back to her friend.

"Thank you, Judy. For coming. For the compliments. For your support."

"Of course, hunnie," Judy said with a smile. "We'll get out of the way now and let more admiring customers have a chance to enjoy what you've created."

It was all going so well. Visitors continued to bustle in and out of the store, each raving about Emmy and Callie Ann's display. As annoying as Callie Ann could be, she really was charming the crowd. And the cameras. They hardly left her side. Emmy wondered what she was saying and also when it would be her turn to talk. But maybe this was a good thing. Callie Ann could be the cover girl spokesperson and Emmy could reap the benefits without the anxiety of having to be on-screen. Subconsciously she reached up to her collarbone and gave her teaspoon necklace a squeeze.

By the time Dixie came by to round them up, they were clean out of candy wafers. She instructed them to leave everything just as it was. The displays would stay up for the remainder of the week and later, some poor behind-the-scenes soul would dismantle their creation. Pierce would be doing his assessments of their tasty displays up at the mansion in the studio kitchens. They were to walk up there now, quickly. Dixie practically shooed them out of the store and up the road, but as Emmy walked, she slowed ever so slightly when they passed the other competitors' store displays.

Silvia and Andy's display was divine. Nothing short of breathtaking. In the middle of Judy's store window stood a mannequin covered in a bold red cotton candy dress. Layers of colored spun sugar enveloped the slim model. Even the parasol she carried over her head was created from cotton candy, wisps of sugary cotton stretched over a metal frame. From the ceiling fell little lines of baby blue paper hearts on transparent fishing line. They bounced off the crimson parasol and pooled at the mannequin's feet. Mirrors on the floor of the display reflected the astutely contrasting colors. When Emmy stopped to stare, Dixie literally pushed her along the pathway, forcing her forward before she was really ready to leave.

Marguerite and Otis's display at the pub, however, was a shocking surprise. Their window front was a sparsely decorated café scene. A small metal table, with two chairs, sat in the center of the space. A golden bucket of now melted ice and the green glass of a champagne bottle sat on the table, surrounded by gold-plated mini chocolate bars.

Gold-colored balloons and glitter occupied the rest of the space. The result was sloppy and underwhelming. Emmy wondered what had gone wrong.

She didn't have to wonder long though, because when she and Callie Ann arrived in the kitchen, Marguerite and Otis were already there, arguing. Apparently, they had been arguing all day.

"Ms. Champlain, may I have a word?" Marguerite asked the second the producer walked through the door.

"No," Dixie said sharply. "You may not. We go live in thirty seconds."

Pierce strode to his mark on the kitchen floor, turned on his dazzling smile, and welcomed America back into the Biltmore kitchens.

"It's been another lovely day here in North Carolina at the Biltmore Estates. Let's take a moment to check in with our contestants, shall we?" Pierce walked first to Silvia and Andy.

"Tell us about your display." Pierce gestured to Silvia.

"Well, it truly was a team effort. Cotton Candy Andy was a dream to work with. I had wanted to do something that connected to the store's clientele and merchandise, so dressing the mannequin was an obvious choice."

"We worked to our strengths," Andy added. "Cotton candy and art."

"The result is a masterpiece," gushed Pierce. "Tell me, is it true those adorable heart raindrops are edible?"

"Yes sir," Andy agreed. "They are made from rice paper. It was Silvia's idea."

"Brilliant!" Pierce declared. "Simply brilliant!"

He walked a few paces down the line and stood in front of a scowling Marguerite and sweating Otis. Beads of perspiration popped out on his forehead, and his usually stylish beard looked damp.

"What can you tell me about your display?" Pierce asked the disgruntled duo. For a few seconds neither of them spoke. Pierce cleared his throat, and finally Otis caved.

"Our display was a classic combination of every woman's favorite items, chocolate and champagne. We wanted our guests to feel *regal* and *special*."

"The chocolates," Marguerite cut in, "are made from organic goat milk and dark chocolate cocoa beans." She didn't sound at all excited about the combination.

Pierce raised his eyebrows and poised to pounce. "I'm sensing a note of discord here."

Out of camera shot, Emmy tensed. She knew what was coming. At least once a season Pierce stoked the flames of a culinary coup. A mutinous meltdown. A fantastic-food-fisticuff. And it looked like this season's skirmish was going down right here. Right now.

Andy and Silvia must have come to the same conclusion, because they were surreptitiously inching into the wings of the set. Even Callie Ann, the camera queen, backed up a foot or two.

"It's clear the display didn't turn out quite how you planned," Pierce said gently to the pair. Knowing it would further enrage Marguerite, Pierce deferred to Otis first. "Otis, how had you envisioned the display?"

"Well, our display was in the pub, right? So obviously it would be smart to build on that foundation. A buddy of mine and I have perfected these hops-flavored chocolate bars. They go great with beer." Then, glaring at Marguerite and adopting a British accent, Otis continued, "They are a smashing hit back in Portland, but apparently not classy enough for this place." Otis stuck his hands in his apron pockets, making it clear he was done speaking.

"Well, I never!" Marguerite burst.

"You've never what?" asked Pierce, fanning the flames. He directed his gaze at the enraged Englishwoman.

"I've never heard such rubbish in my whole life. All day long this buffoon has been talking about natural ingredients as if he were God himself and invented them. Well, I've got news for you, Otis. The people here are *not* interested in your crunchy, earth-loving menu. They want something classy. They want a food, that when it touches their lips, makes them feel royal."

"Well, you"—Otis leaned around the trim figure of Pierce so that he could point directly into Marguerite's face—"are a royal pain."

No one expected what happened next. It was a first for the EatTV competition. It was an event that would forever remain in Emmy's memory, just as Gloria's flying teeth would stay with her forever. But this time, Emmy was not the initiator of the catastrophe. Otis was.

Marguerite took one look at Otis's insult-spitting face and fainted.

Callie Ann screamed. Silvia's hands flew to her chest in disbelief, and Andy's jaw dropped. Emmy rushed to Marguerite's side and cradled the woman's head in her lap, while Otis knelt next to them both and stammered, "I didn't mean… I'm so sorry. I don't know what got into me. Marguerite, wake up. Please. I'm so sorry."

Pierce gave a horrified look directly into the camera, and Dixie yelled, "Commercial!"

When the red record lights extinguished and it was clear the general public was no longer viewing the events in the kitchen, Dixie clapped.

"Bravo, darlings! All of you! Well done!" she crooned. "Otis, you are most definitely going home today, but if I could give you a bonus, I would." She grabbed his bearded face in her hands and kissed him full on the lips. "You were magnificent."

Dixie leaned over Marguerite and patted her cheek. "Marguerite, duchess. We only have ninety seconds before we come back from commercial. Are you able to stand or shall I get you a chair?"

"Are you kidding?" Emmy asked.

"Never," Dixie replied. "Someone from the crew! Grab a chair. Otis, do you think you can stand next to Marguerite without slugging her?"

Otis, who had gone pale and gotten even sweatier, managed to nod. As Emmy helped Marguerite into the chair provided by the crew, Otis continued to apologize.

"I'm so sorry. Marguerite, are you okay? I never wanted to hurt you…"

"Shh shh shh," Dixie shushed him. "She'll be fine."

Thirty seconds later they were all standing in

position as if the ordeal had never happened. Dixie was counting them back on-screen, and Pierce was standing before Emmy and Callie Ann ready to press on.

But Emmy wasn't ready. She was shaking and nervous and rattled and feeling more anxious than she had been for any part of the show up until this point. Shadows were creeping into the corners of her vision, and the beads of sweat she'd spotted on Otis just minutes ago now coated her back, causing her dress to cling to her body uncomfortably.

She tried to take a deep breath, tried to bend her knees, but it wasn't working. She was losing it. She reached for her necklace, for luck, for anything. Suddenly, Callie Ann's voice cut through the fog of her anxiety, and her reality became crystal clear.

"It was all my idea," Callie Ann told Pierce. "A fairy-tale castle, floating on clouds, for the two of us. The dream team."

Despite her laser focus on Callie Ann's lying lips, Emmy could not force her own to work. Pierce placed the microphone in her space, but all Emmy could do was nod.

"I know the costumes are a bit much," Callie Ann continued. "But Emmy insisted. The castle, though? That was all me. Do you have any idea how long it took to frost all those little wafers?" Callie Ann laid a hand on Pierce's chest and laughed. "Of course, you don't! Those silly cameras plum disappeared while I slaved away, so you'll just have to take my word for it."

Emmy could not believe her ears. This girl did not play fair. With Marguerite and Otis's brawl still fresh in her memory, Emmy chose her next words carefully. She reached out and pulled Pierce's microphone in her direction.

"Like Callie Ann said," Emmy spoke with the sweetest tone she could muster, "it really was a team effort. I'm so grateful we were paired together and she was able to include me in her fantasy. It's been such a joy to see her inventive process in action."

"Speaking of action," Pierce said, walking away from the teams. "The phone lines are seeing plenty of it. Voting will stay open for ten more minutes, and then we'll announce the challenge winners as well as which *two contestants* will be leaving the mansion."

The cameras cut to commercial, returned, and then wrapped after Pierce dismissed the dueling duo and crowned Silvia and Andy the challenge winners. It had been an eventful episode, but an anticipated and anticlimactic departure reveal. Emmy crossed her fingers as Pierce announced the winners, but truly agreed that Silvia and Andy had created something magical together and totally deserved to win.

Within an hour of the show's conclusion, Marguerite and Otis were off the premises. The remaining competitors were tucked in for the night, each individually processing the outcome of the day and strategizing their moves for tomorrow.

As Emmy walked down the hall in her borrowed Biltmore robe to the common bathroom, she ran smack dab into Callie Ann.

"Ouch!" Emmy yelped as Callie Ann's toothbrush dug into her ribs.

"Oops! Pardon me!" Callie Ann apologized. Emmy shook her head. She doubted car accident victims dealt with this much whiplash. From one moment to the next, Callie Ann's personality was impossible to keep up with. Emmy stood there and stared at her. "You're supposed to say excuse me," Callie Ann offered as she passed Emmy and continued on toward her room.

"Well, as long as you brought up what we are supposed to say, what was with you on the show today? That interview with Pierce? You know I did all the work on that castle. You didn't glue on a single one of those wafers. I did," Emmy said, pointing to her chest. "And it was my idea!"

"Says who?" Callie Ann asked sweetly.

"Says me, and those who tell the truth!" Emmy shot back.

"Well, good for you," Callie Ann said, her sweetness slipping. "But the cameras were nowhere to be found, so good luck proving it."

"But Callie, you lied!"

"There's nothing in the rules against it," Callie Ann said. All traces of her Southern hospitality had completely disappeared. She stepped toward Emmy with her toothbrush pointing in front of her like a dagger. "I know I may come off as a little flighty. Gorgeous, but not exactly brilliant. And that's fine by me. I'm happy to let people underestimate me. More often than not, it works in my favor. But let me tell you this, Emmy Dawson, do not underestimate how badly I want to win."

Emmy did not know what to say. Had she just been threatened? Before she could form her next thoughts, Callie Ann was smiling again.

"Alright then. G'night, hun." Callie Ann waved over her shoulder. "See ya' in the mornin'."

Whiplash.

February 12

Chapter 14

Emmy knew she was being ridiculous. She was not thirteen, for crying out loud. But she did not want to be kicked out of the competition for the tiniest infraction. And Dixie was practically salivating at the thought of finding a reason to send Emmy packing as well. But...

She just had to do it.

It was killing her not to.

Emmy pulled her luxurious comforter up to her chin and then, after a furtive glance around the room, dove under the covers. There, beneath the mountains of fabric, she turned on her phone. Its screen illuminated the dark space and started pinging and vibrating frantically the second it connected to the Wi-Fi. Emmy fumbled to silence it, and when she failed, threw her entire body onto the phone in hopes of muffling the noises it continued to emit.

When at last the device had ceased to beep and jiggle, she looked at the screen. Twenty-si text messages. Four hundred sixteen Facebook notifications. Fifty-nine emails. Emmy smiled so hard her cheeks hurt. She wasn't sure if any of these forms of communication would translate into any profitable business, but never in her whole life had she felt so popular.

Emmy checked her text messages first. Twelve were from her mother.

Did you land safely?

Arrive at the estates? Send me a picture!

What are the other contestants like?

Hello?

Emmy?

EMMY THIS IS YOUR MOTHER TEXTING YOU.

Oh sorry. Just got a text from Rachel saying you aren't allowed to communicate with the outside world. I understand but think they should make an exception for mothers. Maybe I'll call Dixie Champlain. You father once played golf with her first husband's brother. I'm sure I could get her phone number.

I know you aren't reading this… otherwise you'd be replying… right?!?!? But I wanted to say good luck!

Don't listen to Pierce, your suckers were something special, just like you. Inside and out!

Candy Kabobs! Will you make them for the family reunion next summer?

Sweetie I love you. But please, no more princess outfits.

The cotton candy dress really was incredible. And that Silvia! What a hoot! But I still voted for you.

A few of the messages were from Rachel. *The store has been packed!*

People are begging for candy kabobs. Jenna and I are going to put in a late night getting them made up for tomorrow.

Keep up the good work!

There was one short text from Gloria.

So very sorry. What a sneaky awful man that Pierce is. Please forgive me.

Emmy's heart hurt for Gloria. She wished she could text her back right now and tell her she was absolutely forgiven, but she just couldn't risk it. There was also a smattering of texts from friends wishing her luck and saying they'd voted. It would definitely take her awhile, but once she got home, she vowed to respond to every single one. As she read her best friend Anna's texts, Emmy could just see her feisty face typing away as she watched the show.

Knock 'em dead Emmy!

Passive aggression speaks many languages. Minnesota Nice can kick southern hospitality's booty any day.

Voted! Voted!! Voted!!!
Seriously? You would never pick tulle and
Lycra. The glitter has gone to that girl's head.

Callie Ann is cray-cray.

She saved the texts from Eddie to read last.
Now that they lived together, she was used to
seeing him every day. She'd only been gone for
three days, but it felt like so much longer.

Go get'em Emmy! You can do this!

You looked gorgeous tonight!

Don't let the candy crazies get you down! Be
strong. Give 'em hell Emmy.

Watched with Rachel and Brett and Jenna
tonight. We voted nonstop!

Congrats on making it to the next round my
little shish kabob!

I am proud of you for a hundred reasons, but
right now, I'm proud of you for not knocking
out that princess's teeth. Lord knows I would
have hip checked her scrawny ass a dozen
times by now.

A knock on her door startled Emmy. She yelped
beneath the covers and sprang out of the bed like a
jack-in-the-box. She took one look at the evidence

of guilt in her hand and quickly shoved it between the mattresses.

"Yes! Good morning! I'm up!" she said loudly in the direction of the solid oak door.

The knock came again. Emmy looked quickly in the full-length mirror and made a face back at the bed-headed reflection.

"Coming!" she hollered as she dashed for a robe and ran her fingers through her hair. She opened the door to find Dixie. Dixie's displeased expression—at having to wait, or Emmy's pre-made-up appearance, or both—caused Emmy to take a step back and hide half of her body behind the door, as if she were playing peek-a-boo with a baby rather than having a grown-up conversation.

What does she expect? Emmy thought. *It's 6:17 in the morning. Am I supposed to roll out of bed looking gorgeous?*

Dixie skipped the morning pleasantries and got straight down to business.

"The first part of today's challenge takes place out of doors. Bring two outfits to the studio space and shoes appropriate for both outdoor hiking and indoor cooking. Will you be able to manage?"

Emmy nodded her response, and Dixie left without another word. Emmy closed the door just as Andy opened his. As she went to check her suitcase for appropriate attire, Emmy forgot her phone completely.

~

Dixie Champlain traveled through life in heels. She wore them to breakfast, to their episode briefings, and even to the studio kitchen (although Emmy wasn't sure how they were compliant with OSHA regulations). No matter Dixie's personal reasoning, Emmy found the producer's choice of footwear helpful. Dixie's shoes were a click-clacking bullhorn announcing her presence. There was no need for Emmy to guess when the judgmental woman was going to show up, because she could always hear her coming.

As soon as the sound of Dixie's heels met Emmy's ears, she stood a little straighter and tucked stray strands of hair behind her ears. By the time Dixie came into view Emmy would be standing with a smile on her face. Emmy could tell, under the scrutinizing eyes of the producer, that Dixie was always a little disappointed she didn't find her comedic relief looking very funny. Except that one time she found Emmy in a princess dress... and that was NOT going to happen again. Today Dixie met Emmy and the other contestants in the grand entrance of the Biltmore Mansion.

It seemed crazy to Emmy that she had walked through the front doors of this place for the first time only four days ago. It felt like so much longer. Callie Ann had exchanged her baker Barbie apron for an Eddie Bauer Barbie wardrobe. She wore a buffalo plaid flannel shirt and tall boots. Her blonde hair was woven into a thick braid that draped over her shoulder and was expertly tucked beneath a Coldwater Creek stocking cap. Emmy looked at her own jeans and puffy vest and tried not to feel second-rate. Suddenly Eddie's hip check text popped into her mind and Emmy had to bite her lip to keep from laughing.

"Listen up, people," Dixie called, her shrill voice reverberating off the exquisite marble hall. "Pierce will explain the challenge to you and the cameras here, and then you'll load the hay wagon. I'll follow behind in the car and meet you there with more directions."

Emmy nodded dutifully with each given instruction and marveled at the fact that they were not given a preapproved list of conversation topics for the hayride. Maybe yesterday's unscripted moment had gone so well that Dixie was hoping more would follow.

Pierce made his way to the top of the staircase, and on Dixie's cue, began slowly walking down. As his hand slid down the smooth banister, he began to explain the day's challenge.

"Did you know that the Biltmore Estate once stretched over 120,000 acres? Because land preservation was important to George Vanderbilt, a lot of the land was sold to the federal government to create a national forest. Today, Biltmore claims 8,000 acres as its own. Five of those acres are specifically dedicated to growing fruits and vegetables for The Biltmore chefs. In the 1970s grapevines were also planted on the property, and by 1983 the Biltmore Wine Company was established. Today, Biltmore's Winery is the most visited winery in the entire country! Today's challenge will make the most of these assets. But first, a tour!"

Upon his last word, Dixie fluttered her hands as if shooing a gaggle of geese, and the contestants followed Pierce out of the front door. At the bottom of the steps was an honest-to-goodness hay wagon. As Emmy climbed up and onto the wooden vehicle, she noticed a camera affixed to each corner pole. The familiar wave of heat that accompanied her camera anxiety flashed over her body, but once the driver flicked the reins of a mammoth horse and it began to move forward, they were quickly forgotten. Emmy's attention was further diverted by a cheery-looking man who had just joined them. He hopped up into the wagon and then stepped up on one of the hay bales, but he might as well have stepped out of the same catalog Callie Ann had used to dress herself. Callie Ann must have come to the same conclusion, because she stood up and crossed the wagon to sit right next to him as he began talking.

"Hello, everyone! My name is Jameson. I'm a tour guide here at the Biltmore. During the broadcast, Pierce's voice-over will accompany this footage, but since you can't hear that now, I'm going to give you a little history lesson on our agricultural scene."

He smiled a dashing smile, and Emmy didn't need to wonder at the amount of money he probably earned from the wealthy women who tipped him at his tours' conclusion. The wagon rolled away from the front of the mansion, and Emmy settled in to listen.

"I know you already spent a bit of time in Antler Village, but you might not have made it out to the barn. The barn is one of the oldest original structures on the property. Inside this historic building visitors can see vintage farm equipment and watch trades demonstrations of blacksmiths, woodworkers, and beekeepers that show how work was completed here in the 1900s. In this area guests to the mansion can also pet a variety of farm animals, play traditional games from the time of the Vanderbilts, and even learn, with their own hands, how to make everyday items like butter and baskets."

The wagon continued down the road, leaving the hubbub of the village behind. Rather than continuing to watch Callie Ann swoon, Emmy turned her attention outward to take in the gorgeous countryside landscape. The collection of buildings, both modern and historic, faded into the distance and was replaced with acres of green grass and neatly planted rows of crops.

In the background, Emmy could see the Smoky Mountains. The green and blues layered, stacking one on top of the other. Grass, trees, mountains, sky. It was more than beautiful. It was breathtaking. When she focused on the faraway hills, a familiar feeling of calm washed over her. Maybe, Emmy mused, she didn't need Lake Superior to soothe her. Maybe nature in general was the answer. As she took in the billowing clouds and the streaks of sunlight that made their way through to shine on the rolling landscape, she smiled. Emmy promised herself, not for the first time, she would bring Eddie back here someday.

Jameson continued, "George Vanderbilt didn't just want to build a beautiful home. His vision was much bigger than that. His dream was to create a self-sustaining estate. A huge part of this plan hinged on innovative land and agricultural practices. Biltmore was, and still is today, a farm-to-table estate. Beef, lamb, eggs, chicken, vegetables, fruit, herbs, and grapes for wine are all grown and harvested from this land.

Jameson stretched out his arm in a gesture Emmy took to mean all 8,000 acres. It *was* pretty impressive.

"Now that we have so many guests, Biltmore creates partnerships with local farmers and producers to provide enough food. These partnerships are a great boost to the state's economy and also make a positive environmental impact by reducing Biltmore's carbon footprint."

Emmy sat back in amazement. She loved everything Jameson had to say, even if he was saying it with Callie Ann now clinging to his arm. The Biltmore was so much more than a big ol' beautiful home. As Jameson talked about the solar panel installation and the composting program, Emmy began to think of ways she could take some of these valuable lessons home with her.

It probably wouldn't be hard to find a local source for eggs, and goodness knows Sweet Shores went through plenty of those. Maybe Eddie would help her make a tiny greenhouse on the roof where they could grow mint and ginger and sage. Her mind was deep into plans when the wagon lurched to a stop. In the middle of the field, an open-air market had been set up. Several tented stores were positioned in a semicircle, each offering homegrown goods from the estate. Emmy could see bushel baskets full of fruit, one tent that held tables full of wine bottles, and another space that was packed with jars of fresh herbs. Raspberries, lettuce, tomatoes—a full supermarket of options lay spread out before them.

Emmy climbed out of the wagon and stood at attention, ready to be a good little soldier in Dixie's reality TV army. Her good intentions crumbled when she saw Dixie struggling across the grass, her expensive stilettos sinking into the ground one step at a time. By the time Dixie stood panting in front of them, Emmy had regained her composure. Callie Ann, however, had not.

"Goodness gracious, Ms. Champlain. You gotta start listening to your own instructions." Callie Ann and Dixie both looked down at Dixie's shoes. Dirt clung to the toes, and stray blades of grass appeared to be sprouting from the heel. "You'll never get those back to good," Callie Ann said sadly.

"Thank you for that brutal assessment, Callie Ann." Dixie's face did not communicate gratitude. "Let's move on, shall we?"

Dixie looked at the clipboard she had been clutching to her chest. "Pierce will give you a few more instructions, you'll be given a little time to explore and gather, and then we'll leave here at exactly 11:00 a.m." Dixie snapped her fingers, and Pierce popped into place along with the camera crew.

"For today's challenge," Pierce began in his charming voice, "you will need to incorporate one of Biltmore's naturally grown products into your candy. It must be a major element of your treat, not simply a garnish thrown on top. Your kitchen station will be stocked as it always is, so no need to collect all of the necessary ingredients. Your creation also cannot be an item you have already made for the show, so Silvia, no wine lollies."

Silvia nodded, but did not look at all discouraged.

"You will have one hour to select the best Biltmore's natural world has to offer you. And remember…" Pierce paused and pointed to the contestants.

Together the four remaining contestants chorused the competition tagline, "Life is as sweet as you make it!"

An hour later, they sat in the cart, which was considerably fuller than when they had arrived. Callie Ann was bringing back a bushel of apples, a container of honey, and a bit of gingerroot. Emmy looked at her own supplies and was suddenly a bit nervous. She had almost exactly the same items as Callie Ann.

"Callie Ann, what will you be making?" Emmy ventured.

"Oh, a woman never reveals her secrets," Callie Ann said coyly. "But I can promise you it's good. In fact, last summer it was one of the most popular items served at a local establishment. I've been waiting for the perfect time to unveil it in the competition."

"Now I'm curious," Silvia said, leaning forward conspiratorially.

"Well, I'm not telling," Callie Ann said, missing her playful tone.

Silvia ignored her. "Well, I picked up several bottles from the winery tent so that I can make champagne-flavored jelly beans. I just have to figure out how I'm going to serve them."

"That sounds wonderful, Silvia. I love

champagne! What if you served them in champagne flutes? I'm sure the mansion has some."

"Great idea, Emmy!" Silvia said. "Thank you."

"You're welcome. I'm going to make candy apples," Emmy said. "With a few special extras."

"I'm sure they will be lovely," Silvia said kindly. But Emmy couldn't shake her nervousness. This was the final episode before the finale. She had come so much farther than she thought she could, but she wasn't ready to go home yet. In comparison to champagne-flavored jelly beans, candy apples sounded simple. What if her result wasn't good enough for this stage in the game?

"What will you be making, Andy?" Emmy asked to distract herself.

"Bacon-flavored cotton candy," Andy replied confidently.

"Bacon-flavored cotton candy?" Emmy repeated slowly, not sure she had heard him correctly.

"Yep. People looooove bacon. I selected some homemade bacon bits. I plan to grind them down into powder and add it to my sugar and corn syrup and then—"

"Cotton candy? Again?" Callie Ann interrupted.

"Cotton candy is my thing," Andy said with a serious face. "If I can build a business on a single item, I can win this show following the same plan."

"Well, I disagree," Callie Ann said. "Pierce is going to crucify you if you make another batch of cotton candy. Didn't you watch Season 3? Julianne and her never-ending supply of toffee? They want variety; otherwise, it gets boring for the viewers."

"Well then, I guess we'll let the viewers decide," Andy said and tipped his chin up so that he could look down his nose at Callie Ann.

The rest of the ride back to the mansion was silent.

~

As the horse-pulled cart ambled up the driveway toward the front door, something felt different. Biltmore was a destination hot spot and ever since Emmy arrived, she noticed crowds of tourists, but suddenly it felt almost claustrophobic. There were people everywhere, and it wasn't just tourists. The staff seemed to have multiplied, and many large vans were delivering people who scurried in and out of the house laden with garment bags.

"What's going on?" Emmy asked, dismounting the wagon.

"Big event tomorrow," Jameson said as he helped Callie Ann down to the ground.

"All these people are here for the finale?" Callie Ann asked with wide eyes.

Emmy's stomach dropped to her knees, her nerves hijacking her senses.

"Sort of," Jameson replied. "The day after tomorrow the mansion will launch a new exhibit showcasing the original wardrobe of the Vanderbilts. There's going to be a big celebration for its opening."

"Thank you, kind sire," said Dixie, arriving on the scene. "For ruining the surprise."

Jameson started to stutter. "Oh, I'm so sorry.

But everybody knows about it, ma'am. It's quite a big deal here."

"Well, *they* didn't," said Dixie, pointing her finger in loops that encompassed the contestants. "And now they do. You are dismissed."

Jameson stood for a second, not sure what to do. He looked at Callie Ann for some direction, but the hands that had once been squeezing his muscular arms were now down, and her sides and her eyes were trained on the gravel.

Whiplash! Emmy thought.

"I— " Jameson started to speak, but Dixie cut him off.

"You are dismissed."

He hung his head like a wounded puppy and walked back toward the wagon. As it rolled down the driveway, Dixie barked her final direction and then turned on her heel and left.

~

They met in the kitchen thirty minutes later. As usual, the cooking time went by in a snap. Before Emmy knew it, she was standing in front of Pierce with her creation.

"Here we are, ladies and gentlemen, one episode away from the finale. One step closer to seeing which of these eager candy makers will be the Vanderbilt Valentine's Day Candy-Making Champion!" The music enhanced Pierce's practiced speech, and pseudo audience noises and applause were added in for good measure. When the background noise died down, Pierce dove into the dessert discussion.

"Silvia, what have you made for us tonight?"

"Oh, I am so excited to tell you!" Silvia said as she picked up two champagne flutes and handed one to Pierce. "But first, cheers!" The pair clinked their glasses together.

"Just what is in here?" Pierce asked. "I can't drink it, can I?"

"I wouldn't recommend it," Silvia said with a wink. "But the inspiration item was a beverage. I used champagne made by the Biltmore Winery to make champagne-flavored jelly beans!"

"Ingenious!" Pierce declared. And then, after he tasted the creation, "Delicious too! Well done, Silvia." Pierce set down the delicate glass on Silvia's display pedestal and moved onto the next contestant. When he arrived at Andy's station, his delighted expression morphed to stormy.

"Andy," Pierce grumbled, "this had better not be cotton candy."

For a second Andy's eyes flashed with panic. But then he recovered. "You're such a joker, Pierce. Of course, it's cotton candy. I'm Cotton Candy Andy! And today's creation is adorable as well as savory." He pointed to pink puff balls of cotton candy situated on pink paper plates. From the top of each pink ball, two tiny paper ears protruded. "I present for your tasting pleasure, bacon-flavored cotton candy, and look!" he said, spinning the plate to reveal an animal's backside. "It has a tail!"

"I see," Pierce said.

Andy handed Pierce a plated piggy. The host picked off a piece of the pink fluff and put it in his mouth. Pierce appeared to process, letting his taste buds do the thinking.

"Well, it really does taste like bacon," he said incredulously, "which is a remarkable feat. But Andy,"—Pierce switched his tone and glared at the candy maker with serious eyes—"I'm just not certain that America wants any more cotton candy. I think they might want something different. I hope they are not tired of you and your cotton candy."

Andy nodded, his smile slipping. Callie Ann was next.

"Well, Silvia stole my line," she said, looking down the line at Silvia with mock indignance. "But the show must go on, so… cheers!" She handed Pierce a shot glass. Together the glamourous pair clinked the miniature glasses and then tossed back their contents.

"Mmmm, do tell, Callie Ann. What have I just experienced?" Pierce said.

"Well, we're not done yet," Callie Ann said with a dazzling smile. "Go on and give your shot glass a lick."

"A… lick?" said Pierce skeptically. He peered at the shot glass and then tentatively stuck out his tongue. His apprehension melted away, and he attacked the shot glass like a Labrador with an ice cream cone.

"This is heavenly, Callie Ann. What is it?"

"It's a candy shot glass. These little babies were a big hit this summer at my friend's distillery. Maybe you've heard of them? Howling Moon Distillery? These glasses pair perfectly with their Apple Pie Moonshine."

"Is that what's in the glass now?" Pierce asked, reaching for another.

"Yes! My friend was able to send some over to the kitchen for me."

Emmy's expression remained neutral, but inside she was screaming.

How was this fair?

"But the glasses are a result of Biltmore products. I used apples, honey, and cloves from the open-air market to make homemade hard candy by pureeing the apples and then boiling the fruit paste with honey, clove, corn syrup, and sugar. I then poured the liquid candy into molds, and voilà!

"I said it before," Pierce said, picking up another glass. "And I'll say it again. Ingenious, Callie Ann, simply ingenious."

"Thank you, Pierce." Callie Ann picked up a second glass as well, clinked its hard candy edge to the one in Pierce's hand, and together they downed another shot of Apple Pie Moonshine. Pierce was still licking his lips when he arrived at Emmy's station.

"Ooh, Emmy, what do we have here? So sparkly!"

"Yes, very," Emmy said with a little giggle. "These are candy apples."

"They look like edible disco balls!" Pierce said, leaning down to inspect the sparkling globes.

"I can assure you they taste much better," Emmy said, picking up a knife to cut Pierce a slice. "In the fall we make a lot of candy apples at Sweet Shores, and these glitter-covered ones are very popular with the kiddos."

Pierce took a bite. "It's very good, Emmy. What did you use to make the candy coating?"

"Its base is caramel, and today I flavored it

with honey from the Biltmore open market and a dash of cinnamon. Our tour guide told us that the gardeners here specifically plant flowers that appeal to bees. They even teach seminars to guests on which wildflowers are the most bee friendly, and of course, beautiful. I was inspired. I also added cinnamon."

Pierce looked at Emmy seriously. "This is a simple treat, Emmy, but you have done it well."

Emmy nodded, and Pierce turned to face the cameras straight on.

"Well, ladies and gentlemen, we turn to you for help. Which of these candy makers do you want for a champion? It's time to make your voice heard, and vote! The top three contestants will head to our finale. Make sure to tune in again on Valentine's night!"

The contestants' faces and a close-up of their candy creation filled the screen. Emmy crossed her fingers and hoped that a lot of people calling were selecting contestant number 4.

"Ms. Champlain?" Andy called across the room once they had cut to commercial. "Do you have a minute?"

"I have ninety seconds," Dixie replied.

"I'm wondering about Callie Ann's added item. How was she able to order in a special ingredient?"

Dixie stared at him blankly.

"Was that apple pie liquor stocked in all of our stations?" Silvia further prodded.

"No," Dixie said shortly. "No, it was not."

"Then that is not fair," Andy said firmly. "And this is the last show before the finale! How can you allow her to break the rules when the stakes have never been higher?"

Emmy wholeheartedly agreed and was pleased Andy and Silvia were speaking up, but Andy was working himself into a bit of a frenzy. With his hands on his hips and his chin jutting out, he looked like a toddler about to throw a tantrum. The giant red clock on the wall proclaimed that they would be coming back from commercial in forty-seven seconds.

"It's done. There is nothing I can do about it now," Dixie said. "Callie Ann, in the future, this will not be allowed."

"I'm pretty sure it wasn't allowed from the start," Emmy added. "Didn't you read your rules dossier, Callie Ann? Dixie, I'm certain you have. You know that contestants are only allowed to use the items provided."

"I said it's done. Pierce only commented on the quality of the treat, not on the liquor. No rules have been broken." Dixie spoke sternly, but Andy was not assuaged.

"No rules were broken? Are you kidding me?" Andy blurted.

"Listen, Andy," Callie Ann cut in. "You are only upset because you know you are going home. I tried to be nice. I tried to tell you that cotton candy *again* was not a good idea. Why are you being so mean?" Callie Ann put on a pout.

"I am not being mean; I am asking you to be fair. And I am not going home!" Andy wailed.

"Ten seconds!" a crew member shouted from the wings.

"Enough of this. Both of you. It is done."

In the end it was just as Callie Ann had predicted. Andy went home, and she, with her candy shot glasses contraband liquor, won the challenge. The surprise of the evening came when Pierce passed Emmy on the way off set.

"I know we don't announce these things on the show," he said quietly as he fell into step with her, "but you were second tonight. Callie Ann was the clear winner, but you had more votes than both Andy *and* Silvia." Emmy stopped mid-stride and stared after Pierce. When he got to the door of the kitchen, he turned around and gave her a thumbs-up.

~

At the post-show debriefing, the remaining contestants were lined up like schoolgirls about to be scolded. Despite Dixie's stern expression, Emmy could not erase the happy bubble on which she floated. Second! She had come in second!

"It has come to my attention that our rule about communicating with the outside world is not being followed," Dixie said. She eyed the contestants with a level of severity Emmy had yet to see, and that was saying something. The formidable woman paced back and forth in front of Emmy, Callie Ann, and Silvia.

Pop. Emmy's bubble of happiness disintegrated. How had they known? Were their rooms bugged? She hadn't even replied to any of her messages, now that she thought of it. Only looked at them. Where could be the harm in that?

Emmy suddenly stopped thinking. She knew

she had a terrible poker face. When Rachel and Brett came over for game night, she lost every time. Eddie always blamed it on her inability to tell a lie. She couldn't even bluff without blushing. Her face would give her away for sure.

Think about something else, she demanded of herself. *Think about something else!*

But it didn't matter. Dixie wasn't looking at her. She was looking at Callie Ann.

"I explicitly told you that our photographers would be posting pictures of you online and that your social media managers were welcome to share those photos far and wide. There are confidentiality statements and legal ramifications that you as a sole entity are not prepared to back up, Callie Ann Collins."

Callie Ann opened her mouth to respond, but Dixie cut her off. "I don't care who your grandfather is. First Jean Luc with the copyright debacle, and now this!" Dixie rubbed her temples and squeezed her eyes shut. "You people will be the death of me. Now hand over your phone."

"Are you serious?" Callie Ann said. "You are forcing me to give up my phone for what? For a few posts on Instagram?"

"Forty-seven posts on Instagram, Callie Ann. And…" Dixie looked at her clipboard. "Another dozen or so on Facebook and Twitter. The heart of this competition is about giving a stage and platform to entrepreneurs in hopes of helping them find success. We work hard to give every contestant an even playing field, and right now you are abusing your position."

Emmy was torn. She was more than certain

that the tour date for her store, her nonexistent driver, and her less than glamourous arrival at the estate had all been orchestrated. She wanted to speak up and question the validity of Dixie's statements and challenge if her sentiments *really* and *truly* did extend to *all* contestants. But another, *larger* part of her was so enjoying the tongue thrashing that Callie Ann was getting that she hated to interrupt. Did she loathe Dixie Champlain a little more or a little less in this moment? It was hard for Emmy to tell.

What she did know was that if she looked to her left and saw the expression on Callie Ann's face right now—probably a contortion of arching eyebrows and dramatic lipstick and genuine indignation—she might laugh. And she knew that would certainly not go over well. So, she stood quietly with her head down and listened.

"Give me your phone," Dixie said firmly with her palm outstretched. "Right now."

Dixie's jaw dropped when Callie Ann dug into her cleavage and produced the body warm phone. A small snort of a laugh escaped Silvia's nose.

"You two, too. Give them to me," Dixie said, snapping her fingers. "Now."

"My phone is in my room," Silvia said, no longer trying to contain her laugh.

"Mine too," said Emmy, trying not to sound like a child in the principal's office.

Dixie waved them off and then started back in on Callie Ann. Emmy was only too happy to escape her wrath. She bolted from the kitchen and could hear Silvia right behind her.

"That was the best part of my day," Silvia

said, linking her arm to Emmy's. "Right there. Did you see her face? The two of them. Thinking they are so important. Oh my God, Emmy, that was fun to watch."

"I didn't look. I was afraid I'd lose it and become the next target," Emmy said, tossing her head back in laughter.

"Smart girl, Emmy," Silvia said, nodding. "Smart girl."

After depositing their phones in Dixie's perfectly manicured hand, all three of the remaining contestants headed for bed. It had been another big day, and tomorrow would be another. Even though there was no cooking challenge, Dixie had scheduled mini interview sessions for each competitor and Emmy planned to do a bit of recipe studying to prepare for the finale as well.

As Emmy fell asleep, she was grateful. Grateful to have survived another challenge. Grateful to have been in the top two. Grateful to have the love and support of her friends and family and Eddie. Even if she could not talk to them or read their messages, she knew they were behind her every step of the way, and that meant more than any of it.

February 13

Chapter 15

The schedule of events for the day was laying on the plush carpet when Emmy awoke the next morning. She tiptoed out of bed and brought it back to read while she snuggled under the covers.

Breakfast 9:00 a.m.
Contestant Meeting 9:45 a.m.
Hair and Make-Up Consultations 10:15 a.m.
Contestant Interviews 11:00 a.m.
Lunch – on your own, vouchers included in
*   envelope*

There was also a note in tight cursive at the bottom.

The rest of the day is yours to spend as you wish. Please feel free to tour any portion of the estate or participate in any of our on-site activities. All expenses paid. Do not, however, leave the estate property. Direct all questions to me.

Dixie Champlain

Emmy smiled. An all-expenses-paid day trip to the Biltmore? Knowing herself and her nerves, Emmy saw this for what it was, a beautiful distraction. Sure, she had to get through the intense interview first, but then, she'd be free to wander and explore. She hopped out of bed to get dressed and headed down to breakfast, excited for the day ahead.

When Emmy arrived at breakfast, she could see that Silvia shared her mindset. A brochure of the estate lay open next to her bowl of fruit, oatmeal, and granola.

"It's all so wonderful, Emmy," Silvia said. "How will we choose what to do?"

"Well, the gardens are at the top of my list," said Emmy. "Want to walk through them together?"

"I'd love to," Silvia said. "Thank you for the invitation."

"Of course," Emmy said, spreading jam on thick, oven-fresh bread.

"Why don't we meet up after the interviews? We can grab a bite of lunch in the village and then begin our tours. And then maybe we can visit the winery for a liquid dinner?"

"Perfect," Emmy giggled, "but I think they serve food there too."

The day only got better from there. Magnolia had planned to pull out all the stops for the interview today and the final day of competition tomorrow. In addition to the cases of make-up and vanity table full of hair products, a dressing rack also occupied the room.

"Maggie, what's this?" Emmy asked, pointing to the many hanging garment bags.

"Fun," Maggie responded. "This is going to be fun." Maggie unzipped the first black bag to reveal a dress covered in intricate beadwork. The finale will take place during the opening of the new exhibit called A Vanderbilt House Party. The original owners' clothing will be displayed, and attendees are encouraged to dress up as well, either in the fashion of the Vanderbilts' time or in modern apparel. You, and the other contestants, will do the same. Since Dixie has forbidden you to leave the property," Maggie said with a wicked smile, "the stores have come to you."

"Seriously?" Emmy asked incredulously.

"Seriously," replied Maggie. "And now we are going to play a serious game of dress up. Come on, get over here. Let's try these on."

Emmy suppressed a squeal of delight and started shedding her clothes. Each dress was more regal than the last. Sequins and dropped necklines, pearl-studded collars, and backless dresses. Emmy tried on a dozen or more.

"I think I want to go with one of the antique options," Emmy said. "It feels more… I don't know… magical. Like I'm stepping back in time."

"I agree," Maggie said. "And I've been researching hairstyles from the early 1900s. I think we can make you look like American royalty. Plus, with these jewels, it won't be hard to make you look like American royalty."

"Jewels?" Emmy asked.

"Oh yes. Jewels, as in plural." Maggie used her pointer finger to coyly beckon Emmy over to the dresser where several necklaces, earrings, and bracelets sat in color-arranged sets. Emmy was speechless. Her hand hovered over the gems and could hardly believe this was her life. She couldn't wait to tell her mother.

"Come on now," Maggie said, hustling Emmy along. "The camera crew will be here soon for your interview, and before they arrive, we need to make our final selections for tomorrow. Then we'll still have to get you ready for today. My vote is for the navy dress and sapphire jewelry."

"Sold!" Emmy said and allowed Maggie to seat her in a chair and begin pulling her hair into place.

Thirty minutes later, Emmy sat on a bench in the winter garden, perfectly coifed and made up, with her sweating hands resting in her lap. Pierce sat next to her.

"Oh, Emmy," Pierce said kindly and patted Emmy's knee. "Are you still nervous? We've been at this a week now. Don't you have the jitters all out yet?"

"Well, just when I think I've got things figured out, I'm thrown for a loop." Emmy pinned Pierce with a scrutinizing glare. "Nothing is ever quite as it seems."

"Oh, darling, I'm so sorry," Pierce said with sincerity. "About your initial tour, and my comments on set in the beginning of the show? I'm sorry about all of it."

Emmy didn't know whether or not to believe her ears. Was this on camera? Was anyone else hearing this?

"You know," Pierce said thoughtfully, "when this show is done, there will be another show, and another town and another set of contestants. And with them come more advertisement proposals and network ratings. I do what Dixie tells me to, because despite her prickly exterior, she knows what she is doing. She knows how to produce entertaining TV. And her skills keep me employed."

For the second time today, Emmy was

speechless.

"And besides, once you all get to go home, poor old Pierce is stuck with Ms. Champlain... forever. And if I've made her mad, it's a less-than-desirable experience. I've learned that if I do as she asks, my life is a lot better all around. So, it's nothing personal. Honestly." Pierce forced Emmy to make eye contact with him, and now, staring into his crystal-clear blue eyes, she believed him. "I'm just doing my job."

"Huh," Emmy said. It was about all she could manage in the face of such a big confession. Just then the camera crew turned their attention to them. As Pierce was about to give them the go-ahead, Emmy spoke up.

"Wait," she held up a hand, blocking the shot. "Anything I need to know before we begin? Gonna hit me with any underdog zingers?"

Pierce smiled at her. "Good girl, Emmy." Emmy smiled and released a sigh of relief. She was learning. "I plan to ask you if you are surprised you have done so well in this competition and also review your plans if you win. I may or may not ask you about your fellow contestants, and I will tell you that the best kinds of humans stray away from catty remarks, but witty slams earn the best ratings."

"Anything else?"

"I may mention the approaching holiday and your naked left-hand ring finger."

"Are you serious?" Emmy asked aghast.

"Of course, I am."

With that final comment, Pierce winked at Emmy and pointed to the camera.

~

"Well," Silvia asked Emmy as she walked toward her in the foyer. "How'd it go?"

"I survived," Emmy said. "But barely! Pierce asked me about my boyfriend… on national TV!"

"Well, he isn't the only one who's been curious," Silvia said, waggling her eyebrows. "What did you say?"

"He asked me about Valentine's Day, and did I have someone special I was looking forward to seeing once the competition was over. I told him yes, I was missing my boyfriend very much and couldn't wait to see him. Eddie sometimes goes on big hiking trips, and sometimes there's no reception so we can't talk or text, but it seems extra tortuous knowing we are surrounded by civilization and aren't allowed to communicate."

Silvia and Emmy were now walking down the drive toward Antler Village. A pub, with a sign featuring the head of a St. Bernard, read Cedric's Tavern. It looked inviting. The smells of food wafting out the wooden door were even better.

"So, do you think he is the one?" Silvia asked dramatically as she sat down and put the cloth napkin on her lap.

"Geez," Emmy said with an eye roll. "Do you take your cues from Pierce?"

"Is he?" Silvia pressed.

Emmy flipped open her menu and pretended to inspect the lunch options. Silvia cleared her throat and Emmy caved. "I think so. We've talked about marriage in the past, but we've been so busy lately with the two stores it hasn't come up in a while."

Emmy felt a nervous twinge in her gut. She picked up her menu and finished, "Who knows. Maybe someday."

The server walked up and took their orders then. They split an order of Zucchini Fritters from the appetizer section and each ordered a soup and salad featuring Biltmore's farm-to-table selections they learned about yesterday. In no time at all the two women were satisfyingly fed and fast on their way to becoming fabulous friends.

From the pub they went directly to the gardens. On the way, Silvia told Emmy about her plans to open a taste and see museum.

"The project will happen win or lose," Silvia confided. "It's already in the works. I'm partnering with the children's museum in Houston. But the prize money would definitely help."

"I think it's really cool that you want to connect your work to kids. So many of them will be inspired to create art and food of their own."

"That, to me, is the important part. There is no guidance counselor on the planet who would have suggested I become a food artist. And yet, here I am, making a decent living, doing what I love. It's a dream, and a dream I want more people to be able to live. The taste and see museum seems like a pretty good platform to reach a lot of people and help them realize their dreams can be a reality."

Emmy nodded. Another lesson learned. When your work is bigger than you are, your impact stretches farther than you alone can reach. They walked in silence for a while, each woman lost in her own thoughts.

It turned out there wasn't much growing in

February. But even still, Silvia, with her artist's eye, could envision the way it would look and described it for Emmy.

"It's like a patchwork quilt made of flowers," she whispered. "The shapes and color blocks... they will be amazing. These are more than just gardens, Emmy. These are art."

Emmy agreed. Everywhere she looked was draped in beauty. Lilly pads floated on the pond, topped by purple blossoms. The breeze shifted the stalks of tall grasses, changing their color slightly as they blew this way and that in the afternoon light.

The new friends walked on curving red stone pathways, feeling a bit like Dorothy in the *Wizard of Oz*, minus the coloring of the bricks. They oohed and ahhed over the gorgeous architecture, and Silvia told Emmy that the same man who designed these gardens, Frederick Law Olmsted, also designed Central Park.

"The one in New York?" Emmy asked.

"The very same," Silvia said.

Emmy marveled at the amount of money it must have taken to create this place. The planning alone must have taken years and a healthy chunk of change. But her thoughts stopped when they reached a building labeled the Winter Gardens. Silvia held open a door, and Emmy stepped into a luscious sanctuary. Curved wooden beams held hundreds of glass window panes in place, creating a glass igloo of warm space for plants to grow.

Emmy wasn't aware there were this many shades of green. From the glass ceiling to the red brick floor, all she saw was green. Green leaves, green vines, green stems, and green blossoms filled her vision. She tried to name the shades—hunter, forest, vermillion, sea foam, moss, lime, jade, sage, emerald, olive, chartreuse, Kelly—but quit when a statue of a man riding a hippogriff caught her eye and she was distracted.

Terracotta pots held everything from ferns to cacti. Ornate black lanterns suspended from the ceiling emitted a warm yellow light that glowed from behind frosted glass. Emmy reached for her phone. She just had to have pictures of this. But she found her back pocket disappointingly empty.

Silvia saw her expression and laughed.

"Come here. Try this instead," she said, inviting Emmy to sit down on a bench beside her. From inside her backpack Silvia pulled out two sketchpads and a canvas bag with a zipper that, once opened, revealed a collection of colored pencils.

"I'm not all that good at art," Emmy said, eyeing the supplies.

"Nonsense," Silvia said. "Life is art."

"Said the artist," Emmy joked.

"Go on," Silvia said. "Just make your hand create what you see. Start small."

Emmy thought of the time Eddie took her to paint at the studio in Duluth and shrugged her shoulders. She looked around the room for a subject, and her eyes landed on a fern. She could draw a fern. It was really just a bunch of straight lines in succession. She reached into the bag and pulled out two greens and a brown and began to work. With the sketchbook balanced on her knee and the pencils in her hand, Emmy drew. First the stem, arching across the page, and then the lines that would become the leaves. She let the world around her fall away and focused on the space between each frond, the difference of coloration between the base of the leaf and the tip. When she finished shading in the open space of the paper with a light blue and sat back, she discovered Silvia was watching her.

"What do you think?" Emmy asked, holding her sketchbook for Silvia to see.

"I think you are more of an artist than you know."

Emmy smiled. The women packed up the art supplies and continued on. They spent most of the afternoon looking at flowers from within the warmth of the inside gardens, but also outside and up to the rooftops to view the intricately planned landscaping. Many of the plants were not in bloom yet, but the design principles were still clearly laid out and a wonder to see. Twice more they stopped to draw, and finally, once the sun set, they agreed to be done.

"I think I'm ready for that glass of wine you mentioned," Emmy told Silvia as they left the Walled Garden.

"Amen, sister," Silvia agreed. "We must have done twenty thousand steps today! I'm ready for a chair and a glass of cabernet."

February 14, Valentine's Day

Chapter 16

When Emmy opened her eyes the next morning, it took her a moment to remember where she was. She reached across the bed for Eddie but was disappointed to find only cold sheets. Emmy had been away from home for six days now. In some moments it felt like she had been gone forever, and in others, it seemed that she merely blinked and found herself in this luxurious bed, eleven hundred miles from her real life. For a moment she lay still, staring at the underside of the floral printed canopy.

What will today bring?

She had gotten further than she had even hoped. If Rachel's illegal text messages were true, she had done what she set out to do. The store had been given a boost, and no matter what happened today, she wouldn't be going home embarrassed or in a worse position than when she arrived. She hadn't made a fool of herself in the slightest. She had survived her stage fright, learned new lessons—in the kitchen and in life—and even made a few new friends. As she got out of bed to pick up the day's agenda, she realized she had absolutely nothing to lose and everything to gain. Namely $100,000. The worst that could happen was she could take third place, and third place wasn't too shabby. Suddenly Emmy felt lighter. Energized.

Ready to take on the day.

Once again, Emmy blinked, and the morning was gone. She dressed, ate, and sat through Dixie's dire warnings and severely shared instructions, letting each piercing stare roll right off her back. She and Maggie prepped her outfit for the cooking portion of the filming and laid out her clothing and jewels for the party that evening. By the time she walked into the kitchen at two o'clock, Emmy was ready to do more than just cook, she was ready to take on the EatTV world.

Even though Dixie had shared the gist of the final competition details with them earlier today, Pierce spelled it all out for the viewers at home.

"Each contestant will make one final treat that will be served at the opening of a new exhibit here at the Biltmore Estate. Several hundred special guests have been invited for the first viewing of a display called The Biltmore House Party, which will display actual items from the Vanderbilt wardrobe. In addition to the remarkable and historical showcase, guests will also be invited to taste the competitors' sweets and then cast votes to help us decide who will be the Vanderbilt Valentine's Day Candy-Making Champion. Don't worry, your votes from home will count too, so don't forget to dial in."

Pierce turned to face the contestants. "Ladies, there are no specific rules tonight. We request that you simply do your best to impress us. In the time of the Vanderbilts, lavish parties were the highlight of society life and their guests would expect nothing less than delicious perfection. The same is true of tonight. You will have three hours to make your candy, and your time… starts… now!

Emmy rushed to the storage shelf already knowing what she was going to make. She grabbed her ingredients and dashed back to her station, ready to cook, and, ready to win.

"I can see your gears turning, Emmy," Pierce said, appearing at her side. "Care to share what you are thinking?"

"Well," Emmy said. She picked up an egg from the counter and relaxed as she felt the familiar weight of it in her palm. "Back when I won my store—"

"Wait," Pierce interrupted. "Won your store? I'm not sure I know that story."

Emmy smiled at him. She had told him this fact the very first time she met him, back when she was pegged as the underdog. Apparently interesting backstories about your store were a good thing, and when they'd first met, she hadn't been worthy. As unfair as that might have been, Emmy was thankful for the opportunity to tell her story now. And besides, it *was* a good story. It would make for excellent TV. Dixie wouldn't be too upset with Pierce for throwing Emmy this bone and making the comedic relief look really, really good… right?

"Yes," Emmy said. "It changed my life."

"Do tell." Pierce's eyes sparkled, and Emmy's smile widened.

"A gentleman in Duluth was retiring but didn't want to see the legacy of his store end. His family wasn't interested in running the store, so he gave it away, in a Facebook contest."

"Well, that's the most interesting thing I've heard all day. Maybe all week!" Pierce crowed.

Emmy continued, "To win the store I had to

make up a name for a chocolate meringue treat. The answer I submitted was Duluth Delites—and I won. Anyway, as the store owner, I then had to learn how to make those tricky treats. I wasn't very good at first, but now I can make meringue in my sleep."

"So, you are thinking maybe lightning will strike twice, and that these Biltmore eggs will help you win this challenge?

"Pierce," Emmy said with a wink, "that is exactly what I am thinking."

As Pierce walked away to interview Silvia, Emmy realized that as she'd talked to Pierce, she hadn't been the tiniest bit nervous. An hour later he came back.

"Do you have a few minutes?" he asked.

Emmy checked over her kitchen station. Several trays of meringues sat cooling in the baking racks, another tray was in the oven, and the timer showed she had four minutes and thirty-seven seconds until they needed to be removed.

"I have four," Emmy responded with a smile.

"Perfect," Pierce said. "I only need three and a half. Here, watch this." He handed her an iPad and told her to press play.

On-screen, Emmy's parents sat in their condo, surrounded by warm sunlight and potted cacti.

"Hello from sunny Arizona!" her dad said.

"We're calling in to wish you the best of luck. And know that we'll be calling nonstop tonight. You can do this, sweetheart!" Emmy's mother said.

"And no matter what happens, know that we are so, so proud of you." Emmy's father's voice cracked with emotion.

"Love you, Emmy!" Susan waved and blew her daughter a kiss.

Emmy opened her mouth to respond, but then remembered it was a video message. The screen cut to black just a second before Magnolia appeared.

"Girl, you look like a million bucks, and tonight, you are going to win $100,000! It has been a pleasure to work with you, and I wish you nothing but the best. Kill 'em with kindness, Emmy, and then knock 'em dead with your terrific treats. You've got this, girl!"

Emmy laughed a bit at Magnolia's enthusiasm while her heart swelled with gratitude. Judy was up next. She was being filmed from her store in Antler Village.

"Hello, Emmy! Good luck tonight! The girls and I can't wait to see what you cook up next. We will be watching and voting!"

The screen then switched to show a less familiar face. Emmy knew who it was, but because she'd only met her one time, in person, her presence startled Emmy.

"Hi, Emmy. Amelia Grace here. Just wanted to wish you luck tonight, and let you know that both my son and I are rooting for you! He is your new biggest fan, by the way. Those candies you made did the trick. He got the girl!"

Emmy was starstruck. She could hardly catch her breath before Rachel's face filled the screen.

"Emmy!" she called out from the middle of Sweet Shores Chocolate Store. "We are so proud of you and can't wait to watch the championship episode tonight. Remember how far you've come and that you can do this." The camera then pulled back, and Emmy saw many, many people. Her business partner, her employees, her friends, a few people from the Young Professionals group, and even a few people she didn't recognize. The store was packed. "We're having a watch party here at the store, and we'll all be cheering you on!"

The final message came from Eddie. Emmy stepped back and leaned against the counter. Gosh, it was good to see him.

"Hey baby girl. You are doing your town proud. Everyone here is amazed. Be prepared to come back to Duluth with celebrity status, because I think that is going to be the case. I'm so proud of you, but I miss you so much. Hurry up and win so you can come home! I love you."

The screen went to black. Emmy stood for a moment, reveling in the love just sent her way. What had she been thinking all those months ago when she applied for this show? That she needed more? More than these amazing people in her life were already offering her? That she needed status and prestige and fame? Had she been right? Did she really need those things?

She didn't get to answer the question for herself, because Callie Ann was making demands of her own.

"Did you just get a personal shout-out from Amelia Grace?" Her voice was low, but intense. Emmy handed the iPad back to Pierce, and when she looked up at Callie Ann, Emmy took a step back. There was venom in her eyes.

"You were watching my messages?" Emmy

asked. "Those were private."

"Emmy, this is reality TV. Nothing is private," Callie Ann scoffed. "Besides, those messages will all be played tonight as a part of the episode. So, I'm going to ask you again. Was that Amelia Grace, wishing you luck?"

"Yes," Emmy said boldly. "Yes, it was." Emmy could see out of her peripheral vision that the cameras who had filmed her as she watched her video messages were not going anywhere. If anything, they were inching closer.

"And just how, on God's green earth, do you know her?" Callie Ann put her hands on her hips.

"We met on the plane ride here." Emmy turned her back on Callie Ann and put on her oven mitts. "She had the window seat next to me."

"Shut up." Callie Ann looked like she might throw something.

Just then Emmy's oven timer went off. "Excuse me, please," Emmy said. "My attention is needed elsewhere."

"No, you will not be excused," Callie Ann said, stepping toward her. "This conversation isn't-"

"Callie Ann!" someone across the kitchen hollered. "Your burners are boiling over!"

Callie Ann stopped midsentence, turned, and booked it to her station. As Emmy took her final tray of meringues out of the oven, she heard Callie Ann screech and swear and exhibit all kinds of unladylike language. Remembering what Pierce had said to her earlier, about the best kinds of humans and the way they act toward their competitors, Emmy put down her pan, turned off her oven, and jogged over to Callie Ann.

Her station was a sight to see. Huge pots of overboiled sugar water sat in a sticky heap on top of industrial-sized burners. By the time Emmy arrived, Callie Ann had made it over to the stove to successfully turn it off and was now simultaneously lifting sugar-coated pots off the stove while trying to unstick her feet from the floor. Strings of liquified sugar stretched from the pots to the stove and from her shoes to the floor. It was a disaster. Instantly Emmy's mind hurtled toward the first time she had tried to make Duluth Delites and the relief she had felt when Eddie walked in to help her clean up the disaster.

"How can I help?" Emmy asked.

Callie Ann froze. "Seriously?"

"Seriously."

"I don't even know." Callie Ann froze, with a big sticky pot in her hands and broke another of Emmy's self-imposed rules. She started to cry. On-screen.

"Come on," Emmy said. "Let's move your stuff over here to Andy's station. You'll have to start over, but at least you'll have a clean work space." Emmy reached across the counter and managed to grab a canister of sugar, Callie Ann's already lined pans, and a bag of metal bracketed jewel holders.

Callie Ann stood there a moment and blinked at Emmy as she moved the supplies from one station to the next.

"Come on, girl! Time's ticking!" Emmy said. "I don't want to win this thing because you gave up. I want to win because I made better candy than you."

"Oh, hunnie, that isn't possible," Callie Ann said with a sniff, wiping her running mascara with the back of her hand.

Emmy looked at Callie Ann and said, "Prove it." She dumped the final load of ingredients and materials on the cutting board formerly occupied by Andy and jogged back to her own station. Just as she arrived, Pierce announced the time.

"Two hours remaining!"

Chapter 17

Emmy stood in the center of the Banquet Hall with Silvia on one side of her, Callie Ann on the other, and Pierce in front of her. Three massive fireplaces crackled behind her, warming her back. Despite their heat and more yards of fabric than she had ever worn in her entire life, Emmy could feel the cool air of the massive room curling around her ankles and collarbone. Maggie had pulled her hair up into a regal mass of curls, exposing her neck and upper back. She looked amazing, but even in North Carolina, February could be cool. Emmy shivered a bit and struggled to discern whether it was a draft or nerves.

To distract herself she looked around the room. It was incredible, as always, but tonight even more so. The room had been restored to Vanderbilt-era grandeur. Emmy felt like she had stepped into an expensive time machine and arrived at Cinderella's ball. Chandeliers sparkled, tall candelabras shone in the light of the tapered candles they held, and plush red tablecloths covered the numerous tables large and small. The room had been magnificent before, but now it positively glowed. In here it truly looked like Valentine's Day, but it didn't feel like the most romantic day of the year to Emmy, because Eddie wasn't here. Emmy didn't want to wish away this moment... being here, in this incredible place, feeling accomplished and proud, but she also really missed him.

Pierce cleared his throat, drawing back the attention of the contestants. Dixie counted them down, and then the red light from the camera blinked to life.

"Well, ladies, we've made it. The final episode. Congratulations."

Emmy nodded while Callie Ann curtsied and Silvia said, "Thank you!"

"In a few moments, the guests of the party will enter this room, view the incredible fashion displays the estate has curated, and also, come taste your treats. But before they do all of that, I want the first peek." Pierce wiggled his eyebrows up and down. "And taste. Let's dig in."

He walked to Silvia first.

"Silvia, our creative confectioner. What have you prepared for us this evening?"

"Tonight, I have made the Biltmore guests mini fruit bowls." Pierce cocked his head and gave Silvia a puzzled look.

"Silvia," Pierce said sternly, "this isn't a potluck party. This is the biggest event of the season! Did you honestly make fruit bowls?"

"I did. Let me show you." Silvia picked up a delicate structure made of dripped chocolate and handed it to Pierce. "First I took mini cupcake foils, turned them over, and drizzled them with melted chocolate."

"This bowl is edible?" Pierce asked.

"One hundred percent. Then, after they cooled and solidified, I removed the foil wrapper and set them aside. Next, I chopped dozens of pounds of cherries and strawberries and coated them in chocolate as well. The cherries in white chocolate and a citrus blend of flavors including apricot and peach, and the strawberries in milk chocolate flavored with vanilla. Finally, each little bowl was plated, filled with the fruit bits, and is served with this teeny tiny skewer."

"Well, the presentation is lovely. Let's take a bite!" Pierce looked at the treat from all angles, then picked up the metal toothpick and stabbed a few fruit pieces and put them in his mouth.

"Mmmm, a heavenly combination, Silvia. The fruit flavors are exploding in my mouth. And this bowl, ingenious. Truly a work of art! And I can really eat it?"

Silvia nodded. "You can!" Pierce nibbled on the edge of the bowl.

"Delicious! Well done, Silvia," Pierce said, placing the plated treat back on her display pedestal.

He walked next to Emmy.

"Are these the famous meringues I've been hearing so much about?"

"No," Emmy said seriously before breaking into a smile. "They are better. I formed each meringue to look like a Hershey's kiss and then dipped the bottom of each candy into melted chocolate. Finally, I coated the bottom with flavored artisan salts. There are several varieties."

"Which is your favorite?" Pierce said, his fingers hovering over the presentation plate where five meringue kisses sat lined up.

"I'd recommend the s'more kiss. It is a mallow-flavored meringue dipped in milk chocolate and finished with a cinnamon smoked sea salt."

"Emmy Dawson, look at you, getting fancy!" Pierce said, his eyes lighting up.

"Well, I've been surrounded by fancy for

several days now. It was hard not to be!"

Pierce nodded. "Especially in a dress like that." He winked and popped a meringue kiss in his mouth. His eyes closed, and Emmy could almost hear his taste buds sing. "This is the best candy you've made so far on the show. Excellent job, Emmy." Emmy resisted looking over to Dixie, but it was hard. Would she be boiling mad that her plan to cast Emmy as the comedic relief had failed? Or would she be smugly enjoying the underdog's resurgence? What made for better TV? Emmy had no idea. Instead of falling into a black hole of anxiety and nerves, she let Pierce's praise wash over her, warming her more than a dozen fireplaces could.

Finally, Pierce walked over to Callie Ann, whose treats lay out in velvet boxes. Any air of disaster previously surrounding her had evaporated. She stood smiling, in a radiant ruby-colored dress of layered lace.

"And what have we here, Miss Collins?" Pierce's expression was intrigued.

"These are a new creation of mine. I call them savory stones. It's jewelry you can wear and eat." Pierce picked up a black velvet box and inspected a metal ring setting, with a bright green candy jewel in the center.

"Interesting," Pierce said. "How did you come up with the concept?"

"When I was a little girl, I loved wearing candy necklaces. And now that I'm grown up, I still love jewelry, but my tastes have evolved."

"Are you wearing your own creations tonight?" Pierce asked, pointing to Callie Ann's wrist, neckline, and ears.

"Yes, I am!" Callie Ann gushed. "Thank you for noticing. Here, I made you a special pair of cuff links." Callie Ann took back the ring box from Pierce and handed him another, featuring red jeweled candy that matched his suit coat.

"Well, I'm sure the guests, the women especially, will love them," Pierce said, fastening his cuff links into place. "And now I what, just give these a little lick?"

"Well, not now, silly," Callie Ann said with a giggle. "Then you won't have them for the party. You can eat them at the end of the night, when the party is done."

"I see…" Pierce said. "But, Callie Ann, how will the guests know if your candy is the best, if they don't have a chance to eat it?"

"I'll remind them all to sample their savory stones right before they vote," Callie Ann improvised. Pierce didn't look convinced this plan of hers would work. She was an excellent actress, but Emmy could see Callie Ann was rattled. Today just wasn't her day. Emmy felt a twinge of guilt, right alongside her excitement. Maybe it was down to two.

"Well, ladies, I've weighed in on your delectable creations, but now the second set of judges is about to arrive, the guests of the Biltmore House Party!" Pierce turned to face the camera directly. "Ladies and gentlemen at home, you may begin voting now! I thank you in advance for helping us choose the Vanderbilt Valentine's Day Champion Candy Maker!"

The red camera light extinguished, and Dixie materialized next at Pierce's side.

"Well done, everyone," she said. "The guests will be entering the room in just a second. For the first hour you'll need to stay here, at your stations, sharing your sweet treats with the patrons, but then, once your treats have been distributed, you are free to enjoy the party. Any questions?"

All three contestants, their eyes trained on the massive doors of the room, shook their heads no.

"Alright, best of luck, ladies. And remember, life is as sweet as you make it!"

Emmy couldn't believe it was the first time she'd heard that phrase today, but Dixie was right. She could either stand around and mope that Eddie wasn't here to enjoy this fabulous party with her, or she could make the most of the night and savor the luxurious surroundings. She would never get this night back. From this moment on she planned to make life as sweet as possible. Starting with winning over the crowd. She double-checked her station. In her display pedestal, she had several trays of plated meringue kisses ready to serve. The top of the station was all set to go as well. Just as the doors opened, Emmy leaned over to Silvia and gave her a hug.

"Good luck!" Emmy said.

"You too, Emmy!" Silvia said.

As the guests poured into the room, Emmy looked over to Callie Ann and gave her a thumbs-up, and to her surprise, Callie Ann returned the gesture.

For the next hour, Emmy smiled and served her treat. She told inquiring guests about her Sweet Shores Chocolate Store and Minnesota winters.

She tried not to pay attention to the action on either side of her or what her fellow contestants were or were not doing. She tried to be 100 percent in the moment, making each interaction count.

The hour flew by just as her treats flew off the table. The guests loved the flavor combinations and the lightness of the meringue. Compliments and fancy dresses swirled around her, and before she knew it, the hour was up. Dixie came by, dressed in a gala-worthy gown, and released them from their posts. Silvia and Callie Ann converged on Emmy, the three of them meeting in the middle. They wrapped each other in a hug. Despite their competitive natures, their personal dreams and plans, despite the catty words and kitchen spats, they had lived through something together that few people would ever truly understand, and in this moment, that meant more than winning.

When they stepped back from one another, smiles stretched wide on each of their faces.

"My grandfather is here," Callie Ann said, starting to scan the room. "If I don't go find him, he'll have my little Southern behind." She grabbed a flute of champagne off a passing server's tray and disappeared into the crowd.

"I'm sorry to leave you, but there's someone here I need to see as well," Silvia said. "A woman with the North Carolina Museum of Art approached me about a potential exhibit."

"Go!" Emmy said, shooing her hands. "I'll be fine." Silvia took both of Emmy's hands in hers, gave them a quick squeeze, and then went in search of the museum director.

Emmy stood for only a second before he

appeared. Walking out of the crowd as if a mirage in an oasis, Eddie crossed the room and stood before her. Without thinking, she launched herself into his arms and melted into his embrace. She had no idea how long she stood there wrapped in his arms. She wasn't aware if any cameras were filming or if Dixie was in some corner tisking her tongue against her teeth in disapproval. She didn't care. She didn't care about anything but Eddie.

When she stepped back to look at him, she had tears in her eyes. He gently took his thumb and smoothed away the moisture. He cupped her face in his hands and then bent down to kiss her.

"What are you doing here?" Emmy asked incredulously. "I just saw you on video this afternoon!"

"We taped that yesterday," Eddie said. "I jumped on a plane this morning. Just landed a couple hours ago. Gosh, I missed you."

"You're telling me!" Emmy said.

They stared at each other for another moment before they rushed into each other's arms again.

"Well, who do we have here?" Pierce walked over to the happy couple with two champagne glasses in hand. Once he deposited one in each of their hands, he shook Eddie's hand.

"You," Pierce said with his most charming smile, "must be Eddie."

"Oh, so you've been talking about me then," Eddie said, grinning at Emmy.

"Eddie," Emmy said, "meet Pierce Beaumont, host of many fine EatTV Network cooking championships. He'd already left town before you could meet him." Emmy turned to Pierce. "And Pierce, this is my boyfriend, Eddie."

"Lovely to meet you, boyfriend Eddie," Pierce said. "And what do you do in this world?"

"I'm a store owner," Eddie said. "Like Emmy. Except I sell outdoor gear instead of chocolate. I also put together adventure tours. Hiking, kayaking, cross-country skiing, that sort of thing."

"Wonderful. I've been looking for a little adventure myself lately," Pierce said kindly.

"Really?" Emmy asked and took a sip of her champagne. "What sort of adventure?"

"You know, I'm not really sure, but mansion hopping has gotten a bit old. Maybe it's time to shake off the dust and see what the world has to offer."

"You, sir," Emmy said, clinking her glass to Pierce's, "are full of surprises."

"I tell you what," chimed in Eddie. "You come to Duluth, and I'll set you up any way you like."

"Splendid," Pierce said. "I won't keep you now; go see the exhibit, mingle with the guests. We'll be gathering in about thirty minutes to announce the results."

Pierce gave a little bow and walked away to greet another guest, leaving Emmy and Eddie alone in the middle of the crowd again. Eddie took Emmy by the elbow and led her toward the exhibited fashions.

"So, how'd it go?" Eddie asked as nonchalantly as if she'd just returned from a Target run.

Emmy chuckled. "Good. Really good."

"Tell me all about it."

As they walked and looked at the exquisitely dressed mannequins, Emmy talked and Eddie listened. She told him everything, from the beginning. Sitting next to Amelia Grace on the plane, Dixie's plan to make her the laughingstock of the country, her first challenge and Gerard and Jean Luc's untimely end in the contest, the team challenge and her ridiculous princess costume and all of Callie Ann's two-facing tricks. She told him about her time with Silvia in the gardens and Pierce's secrets.

"You're right," Eddie said once she'd paused to take a breath. "It really has been good."

"It has, but do you know what I'm still struggling with?" Emmy stopped in front of a display showcasing Edith Vanderbilt's evening wear. "This afternoon, when I watched your video message, and my parents and Rachel and even one from Amelia Grace, I thought, how could I have ever thought that I wanted more than that? Shouldn't your love and everyone's support be enough? Am I being selfish?"

"You know what, Emmy?" Eddie said. "People these days have somehow associated ambition with greed, but I disagree. Wanting your store to be successful, wanting to be a leader in our community, wanting people in town to recognize your growth and efforts… there is nothing wrong with that, Emmy."

"Really?" Emmy asked.

"Really," Eddie said and kissed her forehead. "Now, I think I see that witchy woman with the clipboard hunting for you. Better get back to your place."

Emmy saw Dixie plowing a trail through the guests. Emmy gave Eddie a quick peck on the cheek and then headed back to her display pedestal.

"Good luck!" Eddie called after her. Over her shoulder, Emmy blew him a kiss.

Chapter 18

As Dixie counted him down, Pierce stood between the guests and the contestants, but addressed neither. Instead, his attention was trained on the camera.

"Ladies and gentlemen, both in person and watching at home, welcome back to the Biltmore House Party! We thank you so much for joining us, and also for voting. We've had a record turnout this evening, and you've all been a big help in selecting the Vanderbilt Valentine's Day Candy-Making Champion!" Tonight, a partial orchestra, set up in one corner of the main dining hall, provided the intense accompaniment to Pierce's words.

"Before I announce the results," Pierce said, walking toward the three contestants standing in front of the fireplace, "allow me to do a brief review of each of our final contestants." Pierce stopped next to Silvia. "Silvia Alvarez, our creative confectioner, has been delighting us all week. She was an early front runner by winning the first challenge with her red wine lollies and absolutely wowed us with her cotton candy dress window display. Silvia's beautiful, homemade fruit cups were absolute works of art. Truly remarkable in every way, and delicious too! If Silvia wins, she plans to open a Taste and See Museum in her home state of Texas. Silvia, we wish you the best of luck tonight and always."

The assembled audience applauded politely, and Pierce walked to Emmy next.

"Next, we have Emmy Dawson! Even though Emmy was a bit of an underdog in the beginning, she is coming on strong here at the finish! She has made huge progress since the start of the show, and if there was a most improved award, she would win it hands down. While I called her first challenge attempt simple, I can honestly assure you that her meringue kisses tonight were absolute perfection. If Emmy manages to be the comeback candy maker of the show, she will use her prize money to open a second store location, on Duluth's ski hill, Spirit Mountain." Pierce looked at Emmy and gave her a sincere nod of approval. "Emmy Dawson, good luck."

Again, the audience applauded. It may have only been distinguishable by Emmy's ears, but above all the crowd she could hear Eddie cheering, "Bravo, Emmy Dawson! Bravo!"

Pierce allowed the applause to go on for a bit before finally walking to the final contestant.

"Emmy's princess partner in crime, Callie Ann Collins is our last candy maker of the evening."

Here the assembled crowd cut in, cheering over Pierce, forcing him to pause. When the hoots and hollers and whistles died down, he continued. "This hometown hero has been dazzling the screen and charming her fans near and far all week! Callie Ann won the field-to-table challenge and also the Antler Hill Village couples day contest. Unfortunately, Callie Ann's treats tonight fell a little short. The candies, in their metal jewelry brackets, were not easily edible, and some guests reported an annoyingly sticky residue on their skin. However, not all is lost. Callie Ann has always had a strong showing in the phone polls. We'll just have to wait and see. Callie Ann is all set to launch her line of kitchen couture aprons… but first she has to win! Callie Ann Collins, there's plenty here cheering you on! Good luck."

The suspense was nearly killing Emmy. The fireplaces really seemed to be cranking out the heat now, or maybe it was all the bodies in the room that had raised the temperature. Either way, she felt as if she were visibly wilting. She tried to wipe her hands on her dress, but the dress did little to dry her hands compared to her daily wear apron. Her heart beat wildly, and she thought it might escape her chest completely when Pierce began speaking again.

"We've had a wonderful stay here at the Biltmore Mansion, but our time here has come to an end." Pierce put on a pouty face and then let his face morph into a brilliant smile. "The good news, however, is that one of you will be leaving as the Vanderbilt Valentine's Day Candy-Making Champion."

Each of the three contestants took a huge breath and waited for Pierce's next words.

"Taking third place in our deliciously festive competition is…"

Emmy rubbed her necklace for luck.

"Miss Callie Ann Collins!"

The cameras zoomed in on Callie Ann's face. Tears brimmed in her eyes, but she managed to smile and wave.

"Well done, Callie Ann," Pierce said. "I know the state of North Carolina is glad to have you and is looking forward to all that you'll undoubtedly share with them in the future. And now, for the moment you have all been waiting for! Orchestra, if you please, a drumroll."

The drumbeats echoed in Emmy's heart. Across the room, she made eye contact with Eddie. He gave her a thumbs-up. And she knew he was right. She wasn't wrong for wanting more. But she was right too. if she didn't win tonight, she still had an awful lot. A boyfriend who loved her. Parents who supported her. An amazing business partner and a home in a great community. Either way, she was a winner. Emmy smiled back at Eddie and then looked to Pierce, who was soaking in the suspense of the moment.

"The winner is… Silvia Alvarez!"

Emmy released her breath and smiled. She turned to look at her new friend and then rushed to congratulate her with a hug. Pierce walked toward them and handed Silvia a giant check. Emmy stepped out of the way and stood in the background next to Callie Ann, who had given up her good graces and was now sulking.

"Congratulations, Silvia! We look forward to seeing and tasting what you create next!"

"Thank you, Pierce and EatTV for this tremendous honor. Emmy and Callie Ann, thanks to you as well, for pushing me to be my best."

"That's all the time we have for tonight," Pierce said, taking center stage while Silvia stood behind him, all smiles. "Thank you for joining us for this most recent EatTV cooking challenge. We invite you to join us again next month as we make our way to Las Vegas for a cooking competition that will truly make headlines. But for tonight, we bid you adieux and wish you well. Before we let you go, however, our contestants would like to remind you…"

Silvia, Emmy, and Callie Ann stepped forward and together, with Pierce, chorused, "Life is as sweet as you make it!" The assembled party guests again raised a cheer. Dixie let their voices reach a crescendo and then cued the cameras to cut. Dixie walked through the crowd directly to Silvia.

"My people will call you," she said perfunctorily. "You can expect the book contract in the mail by the time you get home." Dixie shook Silvia's hand. "Congratulations."

She turned then and spoke to Callie Ann. Emmy could not hear what she quietly said. Based on Callie Ann's reaction though, Emmy could tell it was probably not something positive. Dixie moved to leave, but at the last second turned in Emmy's direction. Emmy was proud of herself for not flinching.

"Emmy Dawson," Dixie said sternly. "You were a pleasure to watch, and wonderful for my ratings. Well done."

Emmy opened her mouth to respond, but apparently Dixie didn't need Emmy to say anything. She was off and away before Emmy could formulate her response. Eddie was next to her in an instant, picking her up in his arms and spinning her around and around.

"Are your ears broken, Eddie?" Emmy laughed. "I didn't win; Silvia did!"

"It doesn't matter," Eddie said into her ear, and he held her close. "I mean, I know you really wanted to win, but to me, it changes nothing. You will always be my champion chocolatier."

"Oh, Eddie, you are so cheesy!" Emmy said

with a squeal and batted at his muscular shoulders to be let down. When he finally released her to the floor and she stepped back from him, she saw that he held one of Callie Ann's red velvet boxes in his hands. "Ugh," she said, swatting him on the shoulder again. "You went to get one of her treats and not mine?"

"Not quite," Eddie said and bent down on one knee. He opened the box to reveal not a savory stone, but a real diamond ring. "Emmy Dawson, will you marry me?"

Emmy gasped. It was only after she said yes and came up for air from Eddie's kiss that she saw the little red light in her peripheral vision. Just beyond that, she saw Dixie, smiling wider than Emmy had ever seen her smile before.

Epilogue

Emmy and Eddie stayed at the Biltmore Estate one more day. As a special engagement treat, EatTV paid for their accommodations at The Inn, a hotel on property where most guests stay when visiting. Emmy was able to show Eddie all of her favorite spots and teach him all she had learned about the historic estate. Before they loaded the plane the next day to travel home, Eddie was already sketching plans for a rooftop greenhouse and trying to figure out how to keep bees in a subzero temperature climate. Even though Emmy didn't win, she considered it the happiest of endings.

"You know, I was thinking," Eddie said while she buckled up and stowed her carry-on for takeoff. "Even though you didn't win, you could still create that cookbook."

Emmy thought for a second. "You're right. Maybe I will." She leaned forward to dig her journal and pen out of her backpack. "I already have a few ideas. I think I'll jot them down on the way home."

"I mean, it's not like you'll have anything to keep you busy in the next few months what with planning a wedding and keeping up your new uber-famous profile."

"Eddie, stop," Emmy said and jabbed him in the ribs with her elbow. "I'm not famous."

In response, Eddie just shrugged and raised his eyebrows above his eyes sparkling with mischief.

When they landed in Minneapolis, Emmy's parents were there to greet them. They held a sign that read, "Future Mr. and Mrs. Edwards." Emmy rushed to her parents and let them envelope her in praise and love and congratulations. Eddie stood right next to her, holding her hand, and she couldn't remember a single moment in her life that she had been happier than she was right now. While her father drove them back home, Emmy and her mother sat in the back seat, flitting from one topic of conversation to the next. The competition, the estate, the contestants, the proposal, the wedding plans, and back again, doing their best to discuss every detail as if everything needed to be covered before they arrived back in Duluth. Of course, it wasn't possible, but it made for a quick trip.

When the car pulled onto Canal Street, Emmy faced yet another surprise.

"What's all this?" Emmy asked, peering out the window.

Outside her store stood a crowd. They held signs and were cheering. Emmy felt as if her heart would burst with gratitude and pride.

"Emmy Dawson, it is time to address your adoring fans," Eddie said from the front seat as the car pulled to a stop.

"All of these people are here to see me?" Emmy asked incredulously.

"Yeah," Eddie said, opening the car door for her. "Not bad for the girl engaged to Eddie Edwards, huh?"

THE END

Extra! Extra!!
Read all about it!

Not ready to be done with Emmy and her delicious world? Head over to my website for extra goodies! There you will find the Vanderbilt Valentine's Day Candy Making Competition Contestant Dossier (the one Emmy looked through while on the plane), recipes for some of the candies mentioned in the book, book club discussion questions and more!

I plan to add to Emmy's adventures with *at least* one more book… maybe more! If you have ideas of where she should head next and what competitive challenges she should face, please email me! I'd love to hear your thoughts.

Until next time, happy reading, and remember, life is as sweet as you make it!

www.amandazieba.com/read/ccrb
wordnerd@amandazieba.com

About the Author

(Photo credit: Dahli Durley)

Amanda Zieba is a part time writing instructor at a local college, the educational coordinator for a cultural connectivity company, a wife and mother always and a writer any minute she can squeeze in. Just like Emmy, she too loves to dream big and considers no challenge insurmountable. This is her second book for adults, but her ninth overall, the others written for children and young adults. If you enjoyed this book, please consider leaving a review online at Amazon.com. Amanda loves visiting schools and book clubs, so if you'd like to hang out with her, or learn more about her other books, events and offerings, visit her website: **www.amandazieba.com** or follow her on the social media channels below.

Facebook: Amanda Zieba – Author
Instagram: wordnerd_amandazieba

35156557R00109

Made in the USA
Middletown, DE
02 February 2019